MW00526577

The Sapphire Necklace

∞

To Maddie,

Make sure to
sleep with the
lights on !

♡

CdVara

THE
SAPPHIRE
NECKLACE

A Hazel Watson Mystery Book 1

C. A. Varian

Luna And Charlie Press

Talladega, Alabama

Copyright 2021 by C. A. Varian

www.cherievarian.com

No part of this book may be reproduced in any form or by any electronic or mechanical means, including information storage and retrieval systems, without written permission from the author, except for the use of brief quotations in a book review.

Publisher's note: This is a work of fiction. Names, characters, places and incidents are the product of the author's imagination or are used fictitiously.

Contents

For my girls, Brianna and Arianna.
Never give up on your dreams.
Love you

Cajun Pronunciations

Cormier: Cär mē ā

Cher: shă (Pet name like darling)

Boudreaux: Boo dro

Zydeco: zīdə ko

Jambalaya: jam bə lī ə

Bourgeois: boor ZHwä

Ledet: Lə dā

Richard: Rē shärd

Landry: Lan drē

Barrilleaux: Bär I lō

Babin: Bä bin

Chiasson: Shä sôn

Gautreaux: Go tro

Crawfish: krô fish

Breaux: Bro

1

The Spirits
and the
Client

Waking up, the darkness was blinding. The moon, scarcely present in the sky, cast a dull glow over the swamp, causing the moss hanging from the bald cypress trees to look spookily like the hair of a giant old hag. It was almost like she could reach down, pluck me off of the earth with her long fingers, and hand feed me to the alligators herself. I trembled, wrapping my

arms around myself, and tucking my legs up against my chest as I leaned against the stump of a tree. Even without another human in sight, the swamp was humming with sounds of life. When I first moved to New Orleans, I was told stories of the Rougarou, an urban legend of the Louisiana swamp monster. It was said to be a creature that was like a werewolf. Sitting all alone in the darkness, engulfed in the swamp, I was feeling like less of a skeptic. Closing my eyes, I tried to remember how I had even gotten here, but I turned up blank. I couldn't remember anything. Without warning, my surroundings shifted, and the swamp no longer laid before me. All that remained was blackness. My heart dropped, and I panicked, hysterically looking over my shoulders, but I saw nothing but a void. Only I, and the tree stump where I sat, remained. I reached to my neck for the comfort of my family's talisman, the Star Sapphire necklace given to me by my grandmother before she died, but as soon as I wrapped my fingers around the cool metal, it vanished. Unexpectedly, the world crumbled to dirt around me, and I was lost to drown within it.

* * *

A litany of swear words escaped Hazel

Watson's mouth as she dug through at least a week's worth of dirty laundry, mixed with a few clean pieces, scattered across the floor of her small apartment. She had woken up grumpy, due to yet another nightmare, so she was already dreading the day. Sadly, this was a regular occurrence. Having graduated from law school only a year prior, and taken a job with the public defender's office, she had little time for anything, especially not the menial job of cleaning, and her sleep left something to be desired. Plus, her unit didn't have a washer or dryer, so cleaning her laundry was a huge inconvenience. She tossed a wad of clothes off of the sofa in frustration, almost knocking over a lamp, wincing as she watched the near collision happen. Although she was supposed to be a fully functional adult, she lived more like a college student, noisy roommate and all. She often wondered how she had even made it through law school. One thing that she knew for sure was that adulting was hard, and she wanted no part in it.

Ugh! Today is not my day!

She continued to rant, hardly under her breath.

Turning up empty in her search for a wearable suit in the living room, she stomped into her bedroom to resume digging through the laundry in there, leaving a trail of barely audible obscenities in her wake.

"Girl, you need to clean this pig sty," teased her roommate, Candy, from the hallway.

Hazel, unamused, glanced over at her with the best side eye she could muster, and continued her search for a wearable outfit.

Hazel and her roommate, Candy, picked at each other regularly, but there was no real animosity. Even if there was, however, Hazel was stuck with her. Unlike a living roommate she could kick out if they didn't get along, Candy was a spirit. She'd been haunting Hazel's apartment ever since she died there, at least a year before Hazel moved in so, banter or not, Candy wasn't going anywhere.

Candy tapped the heel of her stiletto mischievously, trying to get Hazel's attention, but she reinforced her grouchy face instead.

Although she covertly loved being the center of Candy's world because they were best friends, she still tried pretending to be mad at her, at least every once in a while. She believed their lives needed some dimension. They were together every day, so they had to keep it interesting, and they usually did that by sprinkling in a bit of snark and a few quips into their otherwise mundane days.

"I don't have time for you right now, Casper," Hazel groaned, "unless you can help me find something that isn't wrinkled and smells decent enough to wear to court! We have to stop going out so much and actually spend enough time at home so we can clean this place, before we end up with pet mice, and not the ones that live in a cage."

Hazel, still digging through laundry, was turning red in the face. She finally settled on a black pair of slacks and an ivory dress shirt and smelled them. Satisfied that the scent wouldn't scare away the public, she swiftly changed into the lightly worn ensemble. Candy paid her no mind, and instead looked dreamily at the ceiling, preparing her next response.

"First, why must you be such a bore? Second, mice are cute. Can we get a pet... or at least you get a boyfriend? Maybe, if you had a boyfriend, you wouldn't be so grumpy," Candy rambled, almost too fast for Hazel to keep up.

After finishing her statement, Candy eloquently stuck her tongue out at Hazel, but Hazel was too preoccupied to notice. Instead, she was searching through a box of paperwork next to her bed, trying to find the case file that she needed for the day.

"I don't even have time for myself right now. I definitely don't have time for anyone else. Anyway, I have to go to court", she retorted, before turning on her heel and stomping towards the bathroom. Candy, still looking for a conversation, followed her.

"Do you know much about your new client yet?" Candy questioned.

"A little," Hazel responded, while a toothbrush hung out of her mouth. "His name is Roy Miller. They arrested him for embezzling out of the Waters' financial firm where he worked as the head accountant, but he denies the charges."

"Well, who does he say did it then?" Candy asked, curiously. She was sitting midair, as though she were sitting on a chair, instead of floating in the middle of the bathroom.

"He blames his boss, Raymond Waters," Hazel responded. "Unfortunately, his boss is pretty rich and powerful around here, so going up against him is going to be nearly impossible."

Candy's big blue eyes opened up as large as satellite dishes. Hazel thought she could almost hear the wheels in Candy's brain turn.

"Oh, yea. Raymond Waters is like Al Capone in this city. That case would be tough for anybody, but for you, being a new attorney and all, it's going to be a special challenge," Candy responded, with a hint of concern.

"I know, and it's not like I could drag his boss into court, and filet him on the stand, even if I had the guts. Getting Roy off of his charges will be very difficult and I am properly stressed about it. His 'alleged' crimes affected many people. Many of them lost their life savings. Innocent or not, he's not a very sympathetic defendant, no matter what his story is. The stakes rise once there are actual victims."

"That's certainly not your usual type of client."

"Yea, I know. I don't feel prepared whatsoever."

"Ready or not, looks like you are being thrown right in anyway."

"Yep, and I feel it."

"So, can I assume you're going to be even more cranky for a while?" asked Candy, while playing with Hazel's hair.

"You can count on it," Hazel muttered.

Hazel lethargically brushed her hair and threw it back into a ponytail, which was her usual hairstyle. The million percent Louisiana humidity dictated that hairstyle for her. It was either a ponytail, or looked like someone had electrocuted her, so she opted for a ponytail almost every time. She ran to the door with no choice but to look at her coffee maker wistfully. She was out of time, so she'd be forced to give up her caffeine fix for the morning.

"Have fun lying around, and maybe use some of that spectral energy to clean up a bit," she called back to Candy, with one leg already out of the door.

"Later, doll!" Candy called out, as she waved goodbye.

* * *

Although an introvert, Hazel chatted with spirits regularly. Not that she had much of a choice. Usually, if she made eye contact with a spirit, and they needed help, they would simply follow her until she acknowledged them. Walls and doors didn't matter. Ignoring them for long wasn't an option, although she did often walk with her head down to prevent the eye contact altogether. Some spirits, like Candy, were regular visitors to her. Since her list of living friends was so short, spirits made up the majority of her friends. Nearly every morning, she saw Jim, the newly deceased maintenance man for her building. Jim was a New Orleans man in every way. Before he passed away, he worked maintenance during the day and then played trombone as a street performer in the downtown area on weekends. Sometimes, she could even hear the faint sounds of his horn when she laid down to go to sleep at night. She had tried to cross Jim over, right after he passed away, but he insisted on remaining behind to watch over his elderly mother. They exchanged hellos, and he told her to be safe on the road, because "people in New Orleans drive like they are crazy," which was the same advice he gave to her every time he saw her. He gave brilliant advice, but she always chuckled a little, thinking she was one of those terrible drivers that he was warning her about.

* * *

Hazel's office, the courthouse, and the jail were all historic buildings with their drafty rooms, leaky faucets, and roaming spirits. Since she could actually communicate with the spirits, she didn't mind them. They kept her workdays interesting. Most of the courthouse and jail's resident ghosts had no interest in crossing over. They enjoyed their jobs so much they continued doing them into their afterlives. Without the pressure of having to cross them over, she actually enjoyed having them around, and some were even amusing. In the time she had spent in the courthouse, she had gotten to know several of the regulars.

Those spirits, like Judge Boudreaux, would almost certainly sit on the bench beside every judge that followed him for the rest of eternity. Being in Judge Boudreaux's old courtroom was always entertaining, because no matter what the current judge's ruling was, Judge Boudreaux's spirit always disagreed, and would argue from the bench, although no one heard him but Hazel. It always took everything she had not to break out into laughter in the middle of court. She wasn't even sure if he knew he was dead. If he did, however, it didn't stop him from trying to show the other judges how to do their jobs, although none of them knew he was there. Judge Boudreaux had served the court for much of his adult life. Back in the late 1950s through the early 1960s, when calling your secretary "sugar tits" wasn't exactly frowned upon. He was a large, red-faced man, who most likely died from a blood pressure related issue, or at least that was Hazel's guess. His court-side manner was raucous, so he unquestionably ruffled many feathers in his day. He was Cajun through and through. He had a deep, down the bayou accent, synonymous with areas south of the city. Other spirits within the large court building stayed out of his way, undoubtedly the same as people had done in his life.

Spirits aside, she had a steady income, although not a big one. She definitely worked harder than she preferred, but she would have felt that way no matter what. Being a new attorney, her choices for a position were slim, but she wasn't driven enough to compete for a partnership, anyway. Although she did well in school, she always had trouble with self-motivation, but it was more because of her lack of social skills than because of her impeccable work ethic. Hazel socialized very little in school, so she had nothing else to do but schoolwork and brood. She had spent her life building up walls around herself, because with the constant intrusion of spirits, it was easier to stay alone, versus having to explain why she was strange. She came out of her shell a bit in college, but she was still very much a shy person. One of her college friends, Tate Cormier, remained her friend still, although she couldn't deny that she wanted more from their relationship. But being the self-conscious person she was, it was never something she could see herself actively pursuing. She would have to develop some Candy-sized bravado before she could act on that.

She became an attorney because becoming an attorney was expected of her. Her father and both of her brothers were attorneys. She didn't see her family often, because of the 900-mile distance, but she still carried on the family tradition. Because of the gift she had inherited from her mother, she was already a black sheep to her father and had no intention of making it worse.

Being a public defender in New Orleans was no laid-back career. New Orleans was a touristy city with amazing food, culture, and Mardi gras; however, it also had a history of high crime and corruption that has had an enormous impact on its citizens. The city's impoverished percentage was well above the national average. Most people who were arrested were poor and unable to afford an attorney. Hazel, along with a handful of other colleagues, were tasked with defending those who found themselves in that position. There were always too many clients and not enough attorneys. This often caused those people to receive less than adequate representation, which bothered her greatly. One of the biggest issues she had with her career was she rarely went home with warm and fuzzy feelings. Instead, she usually went home feeling grouchier than she did that morning. For someone who wasn't a morning person, that was saying something. Even though it sometimes made her miserable, she continued to return to work, because she was a glutton for punishment, or because she really wanted to help the people, more than likely, it was both.

* * *

Driving in bumper-to-bumper traffic on Canal Street, while making her way to the courthouse, she watched the digital clock in her car click dangerously close to making her late. She unknowingly clinched her teeth, wondering why she always put herself into such a position, knowing how much stress it caused. Pulling onto Magazine Street, she did her best to parallel park on the already crowded shoulder. She fed the parking meter and then began trudging down the sidewalk in the court's direction.

Walking into the courthouse that morning was like any other humid Monday in the Louisiana summer. She already felt sweat dripping down the small of her back. Reaching around, she pulled her shirt away from her back, only to feel it slap back down against her skin. She was reminded of how much she despised summer in the south. Glancing down at her watch, and seeing that it was 8:05, all she could do was shake her head. She was already late.

Hurricane Hazel strikes again. The judge already hates me. If I keep this up, I may have to move to another city just to win a case.

She took a deep breath, blew it out gradually, and then opened the heavy doors to enter the courthouse. Walking in with her head down, she felt like everyone was staring at her because she was late, even though in reality, it was a huge courthouse, so most people probably didn't even know who she was. In her mind, however, eyes were always on her.

By the time she made it past the long security line and up the elevator to the correct floor, it was almost 8:15. She felt her heart fall into the pit of her stomach when opening the doors to enter the courtroom, making what could absolutely not be considered a fashionably late entrance. The door's hinges seemed to squeal noisily as it opened, before it slammed shut behind her. It may have been all in her head, but she shuffled in awkwardly, trying to be as small as she could, hoping that no one would notice her tardiness. This time, however, everyone was looking at her, including the judge, who looked down at her over his crescent-moon shaped glasses. They were perched on to the tip of his nose, making him look even angrier. She attempted a sheepish smile, followed by mouthing, "I'm sorry," and then she continued her walk of shame to the front of the room.

Walking up to the defense table, she could see

her client, Roy Miller, in the prisoner's box, with handcuffs and shackles, among a few other prisoners who had cases that day. With his head down low and his shoulders slumped over, he looked defeated. After laying eyes on her new client, her heart suddenly ached. She didn't know him, but she hated how miserable he looked and that it was her responsibility to make it right. She hadn't been practicing law all that long, so she didn't feel completely confident in her abilities to take on a case like his and wasn't even sure if she was cut out for such a high-pressure job.

She motioned to the bailiff so he could escort Roy over to the seat next to her, and then she sat down to go through his file. Having only just been given his case, she admittedly had not gone through the file yet. She was silently berating herself for not putting more time into reading it beforehand, but being disciplined wasn't one of her strong suits. Checking over her shoulder to make sure that Roy was being escorted to her, she sighed in silence.

Here goes nothing.

He hesitantly sat down next to her and cast his eyes to the floor. It was clear he felt helpless. She mirrored his sentiments, although she didn't want him to know it. She needed to at least pretend to be in control, no matter how unprepared she felt.

Clearing her throat to get his attention, she gave Roy a warm smile. He attempted to return it, but only managed one that seemed half-hearted, then dropped his head back down, almost like he was too exhausted to hold it upright on his shoulders.

"How are you doing, Roy? You look tired."

She spoke to him in a hushed tone, making sure to sound professional, yet warm. It was harder than it sounded, at least for her.

Roy, surprised by her voice, popped his head up quickly, almost hitting her in the face as she leaned over the table. She tried to play it off, pasting her smile back on quickly.

"Oh, I'm okay, Miss Hazel," Roy stammered sleepily, "I'm just not sleeping that good. Thank you for being here today."

She nodded and smiled in acknowledgement,

but movement in the background distracted her. She glanced over Roy's right shoulder and grimaced, noticing he had spirit attachments. It wasn't all that uncommon, but it could explain why he wasn't sleeping. The spirit attachments were almost certainly draining his energy, a fact that he was most likely oblivious to. The spirit closest to Roy was that of an older man, maybe in his late sixties. She thought that he may have been one of Roy's relatives because they resembled each other. The older spirit smiled gently at her, and she half smiled back, afraid someone would see her smiling at thin air. The man was wearing a dark brown suit, like one that someone would wear to Sunday church. He even wore a hat that had a feather over the ear on one side. She had to admit that he looked quite snazzy. Letting her eyes continue to wander around the courtroom, curious if any others were in the room, she saw another, not wholly manifested spirit, behind the snazzy old man. Although the spirit was only partially manifested, the field of emotions spilling out from it were strong, pouring anxiety and sorrow into the room. Hazel instantly felt her own emotions well up inside of her, so she was forced to look away from it. She would eventually have to try to move those spirits on, because their presence was no good for Roy's state of mind. But, for the time being, she needed to get through court, so she did her best to return her focus to Roy.

"Has your family been able to visit you?" She asked thoughtfully.

"Not much. My father just passed away...," Roy took a moment to gather himself, "and my mom has been real sick. I hope I can see my mom again soon though. She needs someone to take care of her."

Hazel smiled and nodded, reaching out and giving him a reassuring pat on the back. She couldn't promise him that he would get off of his charges, but she wanted him to at least have a little hope.

"I'm so sorry to hear about your father, Roy. And I hope your mom feels better soon. I can't imagine how hard it must be for you to be here."

"Thank you, miss. Thank you."

The rest of the arraignment went as expected, although the judge seemed a little passive aggressive. Hazel's tardiness had not gone unnoticed. Roy pled 'not guilty,' as was commonplace in order to go to trial, but she did not know how she was going to win his case for him. She would have to put a lot of time into research in order to prepare for his trial, so he could have a chance at a fair shot, and that's what she intended to do. Although she would meet with him extensively at the prison, she knew little about him just yet, but something about him told her he was innocent. With any luck, she thought, her intuition would be correct.

Returning to her car that afternoon, Hazel saw a familiar piece of paper flapping on her car window.

Shit! Not again!

She pulled the slip of paper off of her car and awkwardly shoved it into her bag, almost spilling the bag's contents. Having earned several parking tickets in the city, she already knew what the paper was. She paced around her car to make sure she was parked entirely inside of the lines, only to discover she was, so she assumed she had simply not put enough money into the meter. Parking tickets were a pain in the ass, and she certainly didn't have the money to pay for them, but it gave her an excuse to call on her cute cop friend, Tate. Although he may not have been happy to have to get her out of another parking ticket, it didn't mean she wouldn't still try.

She headed home to grab whatever rest she could, and hopefully clear her mind. Between being Candy's sole source of entertainment and pulling an extra workload, sleep was in short supply. If it were up to Candy, they would go out all night, every night. But unlike the dead, she was tired. Also, unlike Candy, she had zero interest in socializing or meeting men. Candy may have been dead, but she certainly didn't let that stop her from trying to pick up men. She wished she could be as carefree as Candy. She always felt so out of place at the party scene. That was Candy's area. Especially since she was presumably the only person who could see Candy. She often thought people must have thought she was crazy when she would stand at bars alone, almost looking as though she may be talking to someone else, but there was no one standing in front of her. Maybe that was why she never got asked out.

Although she wished she had, she didn't know Candy when she was alive. She realized her apartment had a resident ghost when she first went to view it. She figured she would be best suited to live there, since her gift allowed her to communicate with the dead. Therefore, she intended to convince the spirit to move on upon moving in, then she would have had the apartment all to herself. She definitely didn't want to leave the apartment to someone who would be traumatized by unknowingly moving in, only to find out that they were living with an extremely dramatic ghost. They would have eventually thought they were going crazy when Candy would start exhibiting poltergeist behavior by doing things like turning on the television to watch her murder mysteries, which she did daily.

It became clear to her, very early on, that Candy had no interest in moving on. She didn't like feeling like the party was still going on, but she was no longer invited. She died too young to experience her life to the fullest, because she was murdered at only twenty-three years old. Candy was a bombshell, and she knew it. Unfortunately, she was just in a relationship with the wrong guy, and it ended badly. According to the rumors, Candy's possessive boyfriend killed her because she cheated on him, although Hazel had never wanted to dredge the topic up and ask her about it, so she never knew for sure.

She and Candy had very different personalities. Even in spirit form, Candy never left the house without looking spectacular. Her long, fiery red hair was always perfectly prepped, and she always had her makeup shaded in just the right places. Hazel usually wore her hair in a ponytail and didn't know the first thing about makeup. Raised with two brothers, she was never one to fuss much with her appearance. She wasn't an ugly duckling, by any stretch; they were just different.

Even with their differences, she learned to love

having Candy around. Being an introvert, making living friends had always been hard for her. Having abilities as she did, she was always a bit odd, so she never felt like she really fit in. Candy had accepted her wholeheartedly. Even with the flashy party girl facade and the snarky one liners, Candy was genuinely a good friend. She had always been able to count on her, and that meant a lot. Admittedly, she felt a bit of guilt for having such a dependency on her. She worried she was the reason Candy chose to never cross over, although Candy would never admit that. Whatever the reason for her staying on this plane of existence, she loved having her around, as long as Candy was happy with her situation. From what she could tell, however, she seemed happy with her afterlife.

* * *

Returning to her apartment after court, Hazel felt like she had worked a twelve-hour day, although it had been closer to four. Insomnia had a way of wearing her down so much, until she got into a rut that was impossible to dig out of. Not seeing Candy right away, she went to the freezer to see what kind of barely edible food she could reheat, when she heard a catcall from the hallway. She turned around from the cool chill of the freezer to see Candy's spectral form in the doorway. She almost laughed, but stopped herself, when she saw Candy wearing a yellow and white polka dot bikini and red stilettos. Her hair was pulled up into a messy bun with her crimson locks falling around her face, and her dark sunglasses completely concealed her eyes. She looked so out of place, dressed like a sixty's pinup, in Hazel's messy downtown apartment. She put a lot of thought into her appearance, although most people couldn't even see her.

Hazel giggled, clearly amused.

"Well, aren't you a glamorous sight for sore eyes? Going somewhere?"

"Not today, sugar. I've just been watching America's Next Top Model, and I had to show those girls their competition. I'm getting pretty good at changing my appearance. What do you think?"

Candy twirled and winked, complete with a blown kiss.

"Very creative. I like it."

Hazel playfully shook her head and returned to rummaging for food.

"Thank you. Thank you. So, how was your day? See any good spooks today?" Candy asked, while plopping on the sofa. She began flipping through the channels on the television, but she didn't need to use the remote to do so. Instead, she made hand gestures at the television, sometimes graphic ones, although Hazel wasn't sure if those were just to be silly and not to adjust the television at all. She couldn't help but to laugh.

"You know I hate when you call them that. Oh, and I was late for work, so today was kind of lame. I'm pretty sure the judge hates me too."

"As usual."

Candy phrased her response in the singsong way that always annoyed Hazel just a bit more.

"Court was pretty boring. It went as expected. Oh, and my client is haunted, so that is kind of interesting."

Hazel heard the television turn off and realized

she had peaked Candy's interest. Candy had turned to face her.

"Ooh, tell me more. Please let it be a cute guy. Please. Please. Please."

Candy's hands were clasped in front of her as she begged. She looked hopeful, but Hazel couldn't help but roll her eyes.

"Unless you're into elderly men or middle-aged women, you're out of luck with the spirits that I came across today. I think it may be you who are in need of a boyfriend."

"Maybe I am, and you are not lying."

Candy smiled ear to ear, but Hazel thought her eyes may pop out from all of the high school level eye rolling she was doing.

"You're a mess, you know that?"

"Guilty as charged."

Candy shrugged her shoulders and returned to watching television.

Hazel had long given up on rummaging through the kitchen and ordered Chinese delivery instead. She needed to work her way through mounds of paperwork and didn't have time for food poisoning, not that Chinese food offered her any guarantees.

After ordering her dinner, she sat down on the sofa and went over Roy's file, while listening to her stomach grumble, but was all too ready to give up on her work as soon as the doorbell rang. By the time her food had arrived, she had gone through only about twenty percent of the case file, yet had chewed through eighty percent of her fingernails. She looked at her fingers in disgust before getting up to answer the door. She suddenly regretted not sticking with the bookstore job she had when she was in college. It was low stress, and she barely had to speak to anyone more than a few words; it was perfect.

* * *

Before going to bed, she eyed her laundry wearily. She had intended to do laundry again, but another day had passed without it getting done. She would have to go on another treasure hunt in the morning, in order to find something decent to wear, and she was already not looking forward to it. Just the idea of getting up earlier to do it was laughable, so she would have to try to get some of her laundry done after work, even if it killed her.

She laid in bed that night thinking more about Roy's spirits than about his case. Although she had seen two spirit attachments to him; she had gotten a better look at the man, who wore the snazzy, brown, church suit. She assumed the male spirit was Roy's deceased father, so she hoped he could help her with Roy's case. Maybe he'd even know where she could find evidence to exonerate Roy, or find the real perpetrator. Spirits often helped her on cases. They could see things the living couldn't. It occurred to her that his father may have been biased, and maybe he would stretch the truth for Roy's benefit, but any help was worth the chance. She would just have to take any information she could get from him, and consider it against any other information that she could uncover, in order to create a workable defense for him. Hopefully, the accumulation of all the evidence would prove Roy to be innocent. She didn't yet have a plan for if the evidence didn't point in that direction. So, instead of planning for that possibility, like any respectable attorney, she tucked it away with all the other problems she could deal with on a later day.

2

Violations and Best Friends

"I want you to have this," she said, as she smiled and reached out to hand me our family's talisman that held a star sapphire stone. It looked too delicate for me to touch. My heart raced as I hesitated to take it. I knew I wasn't ready for the responsibility of its ownership, or maybe I knew her giving it to me meant she was leaving this world, and that wasn't a reality I was ready to face.

"Thank you, Grandma. I'm going to miss you, but I'm not ready for this."

I hugged her while wiping a tear from my cheek.

"Now don't you fret, my child. I'll see you again someday. You'll see."

She smiled at me, but all I felt was sadness and longing, longing to be back at her house in the hills of Alabama, fishing in the pond and picking peas in her garden. I wasn't ready to lose her. I placed the sapphire necklace gently around my neck for safekeeping, although I wasn't sure if I was the right person to have it.

I sat with her that evening, all night, listening to the machines beep. While in the sterile white room, I watched the medical personnel come in regularly to check on her, or give her medication. Anytime I thought about the significance of the talisman to my family, the weight of it, right there on my neck, seemed to increase. It was crushing. I reached up and rubbed the pendant with my thumb, while watching my grandmother's chest rise and fall as she slept, as *though the breaths would not stop as long as I was watching.*

* * *

Hazel woke up at 5:30 a.m. to the sound of a torrential downpour outside of her bedroom window. If insomnia didn't keep her awake, Louisiana's crazy weather would do the job. It was one of those storms that was too loud to sleep through. Every thunder rumbled through the sky like a bomb being dropped on the city. The flashes of lightning appearing through her bedroom window looked like a laser light show. Feeling like her sleep was doomed to fail, she wrapped a fleece blanket around her back and drug herself to the living room, dropping onto the sofa beside Candy, who was curled up watching television.

"You're up early, morning glory," Candy sang, more cheerfully than Hazel could stomach that early in the day.

"This damn storm," Hazel mumbled.

"I know, isn't it something?"

Candy spoke as she looked off dreamily

towards the window, almost like she had never seen rain before.

"It's going to cause a flood if it doesn't stop soon, and I don't have any rain boots."

"Well, let's hope it lets up soon then. How about you lay back down right here and see if you can get more rest. You need it or you're going to be miserable today."

Candy patted the section of sofa next to her. Hazel, still in her own thoughts, didn't lay down.

"I was having a really weird dream, but it didn't feel like a dream. It almost felt like it was someone else's memory. I dreamed of an elderly grandma giving her granddaughter a necklace, as she laid in her hospital bed. I didn't recognize either of them. It was really intense because I could actually feel the emotions from them."

Hazel rubbed her eyes sleepily, still pondering her dream.

"Awe, that's so touching, but let's talk about it later. Come, and try to go back to sleep, doll."

Candy patted the sofa again, this time more insistent. Her eyes stern, like a mother who was close to issuing out a punishment if Hazel didn't comply.

Hazel, positive she wouldn't be able to fall back asleep, went into the kitchen to turn the coffee pot on. Once the coffee pot was on, she returned to lie on the sofa while she waited for it to brew. Sleep ended up winning her over, pulling her into unconsciousness within ten minutes. It may have been because of Candy's frigid, yet calming, energy that was up against her side, or because of exhaustion. Either way, she needed more rest, so she didn't fight it as it consumed her.

* * *

"Rise and shine, baby bird," Candy sang. "Time to wake up!"

Hazel awoke to see Candy's face two inches from hers, but upside down, and peering down at her expectantly.

"Huh? Candy? What's going on?"

Hazel's words came out more as a mumbled gibberish than speech, as she tried to rub her eyes so she could see more clearly, but her head still felt fuzzy.

"You fell back asleep, sleepyhead."

Candy spoke as though she was speaking to a toddler while she brushed Hazel's hair out of her face.

"Oh, what time is it?"

"It is 8:20, dollie."

"Shit! I'm supposed to meet with the prosecutor at 9. I've got to go!"

Hazel jumped off the sofa and ran into her bedroom. Her heart raced as she realized she was going to be late again. She didn't know how, but she had to make it on time.

She grabbed the first decent suit she could find and threw it on. Not bothering to brush her hair, she threw it in the usual ponytail and headed out of the door. She didn't even have time to pour a cup of cold coffee, so her head was already feeling the absence of caffeine. With no coffee, she already knew that it was going to be a rough day.

Rush hour traffic in New Orleans was sure to give her a hard time as she inched along, knowing she was already running late. Her stomach dropped more and more as the minutes ticked by. Her meeting with the prosecutor was about Roy's case, so she needed to be there on time, but it looked unlikely to happen. Taxi drivers weaved in and out of traffic with wild abandon, something she'd kill herself doing if she dared to try. Thankfully, a break in the traffic made the angels sing, and she was able to zoom into a parking spot. She paid the meter, something she dreaded as her finances got low, and walked into the office with twenty-three seconds to spare. She felt like she may have been experiencing a heart attack, and her hair was frizzed out like a tumbleweed, but at least she wasn't late. She let out a sigh of relief.

Why do I always do this to myself?

Meeting with prosecutors was always intimidating whenever she had a client that had been charged with a serious crime. Being a still fairly new attorney, she didn't have a good game face yet. She still had more of a deer in the headlights look, and they could surely still see her sweat. It was bad enough she was petite and mousy, and not exactly an intimidating looking individual, but her lack of confidence made it that much harder for her to speak up for herself. She needed to work extra hard to get exactly as far as the next guy, or girl, but she wasn't sure what it would take for her to build up the kind of confidence she needed to exceed in her chosen career field.

The prosecutor, Benjamin Reeves, called her into the meeting room, which was a relatively small room with a circular table, and placed a large folder of paperwork in front of her. She spent close to two hours with him as he went over the plea deal offer with her, as well as the evidence against Roy. When she took her leave, she had a lot to think about, and to discuss with Roy. The prosecutor had offered a plea deal, but she knew it would be a terrible deal for Roy because she truly believed him to be innocent. But bad deal or not, she still needed to present it to him. It wasn't her decision to make.

On the way to the prison, she contemplated the deal that was offered to Roy. She felt like it was a step away from being the equivalent to highway robbery. Twenty years in prison for the crime without him even having a record was ludicrous. The more she thought about making the offer to Roy, the more nauseated she became. It made little sense for him to be given such a steep sentence. It sickened her to wonder if Roy's wealthy boss, Raymond Waters, had his slimy tentacles inside of the justice system, and if he was the one putting pressure on the prosecutor to throw the book at Roy. It wasn't like corruption was new to The Big Easy.

She arrived at the prison shortly after leaving the prosecutor's office. She hoped to meet with Roy quickly, because the lack of sleep was really catching up with her, and she was beginning to feel like she could no longer concentrate. If she didn't go home and get some real sleep, she would eventually lose the ability to function altogether.

She pulled on her jacket, as she walked into the prison conference room, because just from the chill emanating through the doorway, she knew Roy had spirits with him. In her hand, she held a file folder containing the plea deal offer meant for him. Roy was already sitting in the conference room, handcuffed and shackled to the table. Her heart dropped, as it always did, when she saw him in that state. As was often the case, he looked unwell. His eyes were barely open above dark bags, and his face was drawn. She hated to think his father's spirit would drain his energy to this level, but she believed that both spirits, combined with the stresses of prison life, altogether were tearing him down piece by piece. With him in the state he was in, she dreaded even mentioning the terms of the plea deal to him.

"Good morning, Roy."

She smiled warmly as she sat down at the table. He nodded in her direction.

"Good morning, Miss Hazel."

Roy's deceased father was still there, by his side, just as he had been in court, but Roy harbored the other spirt as well, the spirit she only saw briefly while in court. Only partially manifested, as it was in court, she could not make out many details about the second spirit haunting Roy. She thought she could make out a long skirt and high-heeled shoes, but that was all she had to go on. Based on the clothing, she believed the spirit to be a woman, at least that was all she could guess. All she could see was a vague impression of the spirit's form, almost like a fuzzy disturbance between worlds, so she wasn't totally sure about her analysis. Unlike most spirits she had helped in her life, the spirit in the room's corner did not seem to want to make contact with her, or maybe it was unable to. Not all spirits were as powerful as Candy, so it wasn't unreasonable to believe this one to be weaker in its abilities. She wasn't sure of its intentions, but the less it showed itself to her, and the more it didn't communicate with her, the more curious she was about why it was there. One thing she got from the second spirit was the intense emotions radiating off of it, which spilled grief and uncertainty into the room like a gas leak. She could feel her own mind begin to play tricks on her as the emotions of the spirit intertwined with her own. It took all of her willpower to pull her attention away from the mysterious spirit. But, realizing that Roy was staring at her, perhaps wondering why she had trailed off, she promptly returned her attention to him.

"Sorry for getting lost in my thoughts. I am here this morning because I met with the prosecutor a few hours ago, and they had a plea deal for you. You and I have a meeting scheduled for tomorrow, where we will have the conference room for more time. I plan to get your full account of events then, but I wanted to run this by you today."

Tilting his head up, Roy nodded in acknowledgement.

He's not feeling very sociable today... that spirit's emotions are affecting him more than I thought. That's not good.

She hesitated, but opened the folder to reveal its contents. Just the motion caused her to be filled with dread, or maybe it was the toxic emotions of the spirit in the corner. She could no longer differentiate from its emotions and her own. Although she wanted to snap the folder closed, and protect Roy from the fate that was inside, she couldn't do that. He leaned in to see it better, giving her no choice but to push the papers closer to him, revealing the unreasonable plea deal.

"Roy, before I go over the plea deal, I have to tell you that I don't like it. It is their first offer. I didn't have a choice but to show it to you, but I wanted to make sure you knew my opinion about it. We still have time to figure this case out and try to prove your innocence. If you take this deal, you're agreeing to twenty years in prison, and that's with no trial. You'll get no chance to fight this at all."

Roy winced, closing his eyes tight for a moment. Hazel sat quietly, letting him absorb the decision she had given to him. She knew it wasn't really a decision at all, but it was the only one he had. It wasn't even her future at stake, and even she was feeling queasy.

After a few minutes of no one speaking, she knew she had to force the decision from him, although she didn't want to.

"Roy," she said, interrupting his thoughts.

He returned his gaze to her and she could see the fear in his eyes. The pressure of his future made her chest tighten into a knot, and it filled her with uncertainty.

"Miss Hazel... I can't take this deal."

His voice was hesitant, as though even he was unsure of what decision he should make.

She nodded her head in agreement. A bit of calming warmth poured over her, where the knot had earlier been. Although she knew it wouldn't be an easy case, accepting the plea deal would have given her no chance to help Roy. They both needed a chance to prove his innocence, so she was relieved they were on the same page.

"I know you can't. I wouldn't expect you to."

Before leaving the conference room, she put out the paperwork for him to sign in order to formally reject the plea agreement. She was relieved to have the dreaded conversation over with. Her day had already been long, so she wanted nothing more than to go home.

* * *

Upon arriving home, she found Candy sprawled out on the sofa, watching her usual murder mysteries. Candy popped up when she opened the door and ran over to her like a pet

Shih Tzu who had missed her owner all day. Hazel didn't know whether to be annoyed or flattered.

"Awe, did you miss me, Candy?"

She teased Candy playfully, reaching out to mess up her hair, but Candy ducked out of the way. Candy's crimson hair was so long that it made Hazel slightly envious, although she would never want the responsibility of washing it.

Candy sat on the countertop as Hazel unloaded all of her belongings, throwing off her shoes and keys by the door, knowing that she wouldn't be able to find her keys by the morning. She had always meant to get a little hook for the wall, but she never remembered when it was convenient.

"It's boring being home all day by myself, and you won't let me go to work with you, so..." Candy whined.

Hazel ignored her, turning to dig in the refrigerator, already knowing she would find nothing to eat in there.

"That is correct. You are too distracting to come to work with me. I'm sorry that you're bored, but you can always go out and find someone else to annoy. Maybe get a job at a haunted attraction? Oh, or you could find a ghost boyfriend. Didn't you just tell me to get a boyfriend a few days ago?"

Hazel smirked but Candy looked at her like she was crazy, sighed loudly, and then dematerialized, only to re-materialize across the room and back on the sofa. It was her version of a mini tantrum, spirit style. Turning the television back on with some choice hand signals, Candy sunk into a show about serial killers. For a murder victim, she certainly had an unhealthy obsession with murder mysteries. Hazel watched her in amusement. She was absolutely positive that some of those hand gestures were meant solely for her.

Settling on a peanut butter and jelly sandwich, since living like a college student was kind of her thing, she sat down on the sofa right next to Candy, who did her best to ignore her. They took the dimension in their relationship seriously, and ignoring each other was an integral part of the landscape. Refusing to play along, Hazel cleared her throat.

"Doesn't watching this stuff all the time stress you out?"

Candy shrugged.

"I don't know. I guess I'm just curious what people who do this to others are thinking. Like... what is in the mind of a killer? I just don't understand it, so I keep hoping that one day I will."

Hazel hadn't been expecting an answer at all, and she definitely wasn't expecting that answer. She found herself with no words to respond. She admittedly did her best to avoid thinking about Candy's murder. It was just too painful otherwise. She loved Candy, and she also wondered what could have driven someone to take her life, but no reason would have been reason enough to justify such an action.

Even not understanding Candy's fascination with the mode in which she was killed, Hazel still stayed up and watched television with her for a few hours while she did some overdue laundry. She watched so many murder mysteries that she felt a bit frazzled by the time she went to bed. Lying in bed that night, she spent a few hours reading about the psychological profiles of serial killers. It was the best bedtime reading material if you wanted to lie in bed, becoming more disturbed, versus more relaxed. Although it would have benefited her to abort her research, she found the topic to be intriguing, so she kept on until she had become so exhausted that she had nearly dropped her phone on her face. At that point, to save herself from a broken tooth or a black eye, she put her phone down and tried to go to sleep.

* * *

"Get into the trunk of my car," he snarled while holding a gun only inches from my face.

I had no choice but to obey. If I made a scene, he would kill me. The entire thing happened so fast. I only intended to go to dinner. I didn't understand what was happening. Why was he doing this? All I could think about was my life was over.

Getting into the trunk, I didn't know where I was going, but once the car stopped, a sharp pain caused me to fall into darkness.

* * *

Hazel woke up in a cold sweat. The nightmares were getting more vivid, and she didn't know how to stop them.

Pulling off her eye mask, so she could see if it was daylight yet, she noticed a shadow near the edge of her bed. She squinted against the darkness as she reached a trembling hand towards her bedside table to turn on the lamp. Heart still racing from the intensity of the nightmare, she noticed movement in the darkness. The light flickered for just a moment and then the bulb shattered. The shadow moved closer yet again. Tilting her head to one side and furrowing her brow, she felt her chest tighten as she tried to decipher the obscurity.

"Candy? Is that you?"

Hazel's voice came out shaky. She heard no response.

"Candy, if that is you, this isn't funny."

As soon as she spoke it out loud, she realized it could not have been Candy, because, although Candy was every bit of a joker, Candy knew she struggled with nightmares, and Candy cared enough about her not to do anything to make those worse. She swallowed against the growing lump in her throat.

"Who are you? Please show yourself."

An uncomfortable chill ran throughout her body as she made demands she instantly regretted.

As though turning on an internal light switch, the spirit of a woman became visible only a few feet away from her. It was the same spirit she had seen at the courthouse. The same spirit she had seen in the corner of the prison conference room that very day. Although she had never gotten a good look at the spirit before, she had an unshakeable feeling it was the same entity because its potent emotions were already spreading all over her body, like a rash she couldn't itch. The confusion and sadness were palpable, and she could feel her own tears building, even though she wasn't someone who cried often. The spirit opened her mouth, in what looked to be a scream, but no sound came out. Before Hazel had a chance to react, the spirit vanished.

Nearly sick to her stomach, and fighting to calm her shallow breathing, she made her way to the wall and forcefully flipped on the light switch before dropping to the floor. She pulled her knees up under her chin as her entire body trembled. The spirit was gone, but she still felt its chill in the air, and the sorrow and uncertainty it had left behind. She wrapped her arms firmly around her legs to protect herself from it, and to comfort herself when there was no one else there to do it. She didn't know where Candy was, but she wished she hadn't been alone. It was times like these where her abilities felt more like a curse than a gift.

Spirits typically came to her for help, and she was used to that, but this encounter was unusual. She seldom came across a spirit who haunted but didn't want to make the reason known. Maybe the spirit wanted to speak to her but couldn't. Thoughts continued to race in her head as she concentrated on slowing down her breathing. She didn't understand what had just happened, which made her feel insurmountable anxiety.

"If I'd known that you were still awake, I would've asked you to tear up the town with me, doll."

Candy fluttered into Hazel's bedroom, practically swooning, but her smile faded as she finally turned her gaze down and noticed Hazel crumpled on the floor.

"Oh no, doll! Are you okay? What happened?"

Candy rushed over to Hazel's side and grabbed her face with two icy hands. She lifted Hazel's face, so she could examine it, making sure her friend was unharmed. As soon as it satisfied her that Hazel was not physically hurt, she dropped beside her and draped an arm over her back. Hazel could feel her nerves relaxing as Candy transferred soothing energy to her.

"You gave me quite a fright, love. Why are you curled up here on the floor? It's an odd place to be in the middle of the night."

Still feeling so much confusion, it took her a moment to gather herself. After a few deep breaths, she leaned her back up against the wall. She didn't know what to make of the visit, since she did not know what the spirit had come to her for.

"Remember how I told you that my new client had two entity attachments, one who I believed to be his father but there was another I thought might be a woman?"

"Yes, I remember."

"I'm not sure why, but it seems the woman must have followed me home from the prison yesterday, or today... I don't even know what time it is."

She tried to lean up to see the clock on her nightstand, but Candy gently pushed her back down, wrapping her in a cool, gentle pressure.

"The time doesn't matter, love. Did she say anything?"

"She never manifested herself before I went to bed, so I don't think she showed until later. I woke up a little while ago, for some strange reason. I guess I felt like there was a presence watching me or something. So, I got pretty spooked and then I saw her. I thought she was going to speak to me, but when she opened her mouth, into what looked like a scream, she just vanished. I've never experienced anything like that. Her emotions became a part of me. I couldn't protect myself from them. It was like she took over my body."

Candy's mouth hung open, as though she were watching a horror film and waiting for the young girl to get massacred down the dark alley, as they always did, because they never seemed to stay inside where it's safe.

"Wow, Hazel, I would have peed in my pants. I'm so sorry I wasn't here, and you had to go through that alone."

"I think I may have. It's okay. I'm okay now. I just hope she doesn't do that again. Maybe I should try to go to the prison again and see if I can get her to talk to me?"

"That sounds like a good plan, love. She needs boundaries. They shouldn't be able to just come into our home like that. Maybe you should check with one of those Voodoo priestesses in the city or something and see if there are ways to keep them out of our private space. There must be something we can do to protect our home."

"I'm not sure if I want to dabble in that type of

stuff, but I'll do a little research. As far as setting boundaries for her, that's easy to say, but if I can't hear her, I'm not even sure if she can hear me. I can try though."

"Well, that's all you can do. But for now, get yourself some more beauty sleep. You look dreadful."

Knowing that Candy had a point, she shrugged the incident off, and did her best to put it in the back of her mind. It would not do her any good to continue to dwell on it anymore that night, or morning, since she still didn't know the time.

Candy reached out a hand to help Hazel lift herself off of the ground. Her teeth chattered against the chill of Candy's grip. Still a little shaky, she used the wall as a brace with her other hand.

"Candy, can you stay with me while I sleep, just in case she comes back?"

"Well, of course, love, what are friends for?"

Candy climbed into the queen-sized bed next to her and leaned up against her back. Although Candy's proximity caused a cold that Hazel could feel in her bones, it comforted her. It made her feel safe.

With no way for her to know why the female spirit was haunting Roy, or why it had showed up in her bedroom, she realized all she could do was try to contact it again, and hope the spirit was receptive. She understood she would almost certainly have to go to the prison to see the woman again, but she certainly preferred that to having the spirit return for another nightly visit in her bedroom.

Just in case the spirit returned, however, Candy was watching over her. So, with Candy against her back, lightly petting her hair, she fell back asleep.

3

The Prisoner and the Secretary

Hazel woke up still shaken from her experience with the female spirit who traumatized her in the middle of the night. She felt like she may lose her mind from all the sleepless nights she had suffered in the recent weeks. She had helped countless spirits in her life, and they almost always had an agenda, but they usually made their agendas known to her quickly. Sometimes, they simply needed help to cross over to the other side. Other times, they may have had unfinished business and needed her to contact a loved one. Although those were the situations she dreaded, because it usually ended with someone thinking she was insane. People didn't usually take the 'I see ghosts' claim well, at least not in her experience. But, no matter what, she always tried to help them. It was what she was born to do, so she couldn't turn her back on them. This case, however, with this spirit, had her perplexed. She didn't know what it wanted, if it could communicate with her at all, or if it even wanted to communicate with her. If it didn't want to communicate with her, then why was it showing up at her house? Why was it following her client? Feeling more confused than she had ever felt about a spirit, she knew she had to try to speak to it again if she was going to understand what it wanted. The situation was going to stress her out until she was able to get answers.

Throwing off her covers and grabbing her cell off the bedside table, a headache already throbbed in her head. It was just another symptom of her never-ending insomnia. The headaches came more often as her sleep got progressively worse. She wished the weekends brought some solace, but the nightmares hit her there too, so she seemed to have no break from it.

Squinting her eyes against the brightness of her phone screen, she scrolled through her phone's contact list to the entry for the prison, and then put in a call in to verify her scheduled meeting with Roy. Hopefully, with any luck, the mysterious spirit would find her voice by 11 a.m. That was what time she needed to be back in the conference room.

"Morning, sunshine. How did you sleep?"

Candy came into the bedroom and plopped onto the bed. As always, she was dressed to the nines in a plum-colored mini dress and black pumps. Her rich red hair was left down and flowing against her back. She had gotten really skilled at changing her appearance. For a spirit, she had become quite powerful. It reminded Hazel of why she never wanted to get on Candy's bad side. Her poltergeist abilities were top notch. She had seen it firsthand when first viewing the apartment. At the time, Candy didn't realize that Hazel could see her, so she tried to scare Hazel off by throwing things around and messing with the electronics. Clearly it had not worked, because Hazel moved in only a week later, to the realtor's delight.

"As good as could be expected. I have a meeting with Roy at 11. Hopefully she's there, and I am able to talk to her. That gives me just under two hours to get ready and eat some breakfast."

"Please tell me you're going to wash your hair, honey. You are quite the greaseball, a cute one though."

Candy frowned, using her recently licked finger to tame one of Hazel's flyaway eyebrows. Hazel cringed and then stuck out her tongue dramatically.

"Eww... and I know. Washing my hair is like a full-time job. Maybe I'll just shave it off."

Hazel flopped back on the bed in resignation.

"Oh, but luscious locks are so sexy. Tate certainly likes them. I can tell."

Candy gushed seductively, wiggling her eyebrows before flashing a devilish smile.

Instead of responding, Hazel rolled her eyes before stomping into the bathroom, slamming the door in her wake. Their friendship sometimes took on the characteristics of two middle-schoolers.

The warm water felt good on her exhausted body. The headache still pounded in her head as she craved coffee. She caught herself thinking of Tate. Candy always insisted he wanted to be with her, but she never imagined she could ever be good enough for him. Plus, he did not know she could speak to the dead, and she couldn't risk telling him and having him think she was crazy. He deserved to be with a girl with normal talents, like ballet, or even ventriloquism. She couldn't deny her feelings for him though, at least not to herself.

Pushing her thoughts aside, she turned the water off, wrapped a towel around her head, and haphazardly dried herself off. As she wiped the condensation off the mirror, a ghostly face appeared in the reflection, standing right behind her. A man, who looked to be in his mid-twenties, shivered as he dripped bloody water onto her bathroom floor. From what she could see, he appeared to have several bleeding wounds on the front of his body, and looked as though he had been stabbed. Stunned, she turned around to face him, but by the time she met his direction, he was gone. Slightly shaken and confused, she fled the room. She only had time for one mysterious ghost at a time, so the man in the mirror would have to wait his turn. Plus, she needed coffee in her as soon as possible. The grumpy mood was growing, so she got dressed and tried to move on with her day.

"I put the coffee on for you, love." Candy called out from the kitchen.

"Thank you! You're amazing sometimes," Hazel yelled back as she crossed down the hall from her bedroom into the open kitchen and living room area.

Her living room still looked much like the day before. Although she had gotten some of her laundry done, the room was still in urgent need of a cleaning. Her apartment looked like it belonged to a young college student who did way too much partying, and snubbed all of their responsibilities, but had rich parents who always bailed them out. However, she had little money, so she didn't have that excuse. The smell of coffee made her feel a bit more alive as it filled her nostrils. She filled her mug and popped a few waffles into the toaster.

While waiting for her breakfast of champions, she walked over to take the spot on the sofa next to Candy. Grabbing the remote, she switched it from Candy's murder mysteries to The Weather Channel. It was important to monitor the weather in the summer and fall months in South Louisiana because of hurricane season. New Orleans was drastically below sea level, so they would have to evacuate the city for any flooding storms, even for something substantially less than a hurricane. Looking at the television screen, she saw two of the infamous swirling blotches that circled in the Atlantic Ocean. Those swirling blotches were some sort of tropical disturbance, and the tracks of the storms wouldn't be known until they were much closer to making landfall. It was always a waiting game to see who won the prize and got the storm. It was like playing darts. She just hoped they didn't land on her.

"I hope we don't have to evacuate this year. I don't have the time or the money. The entire ordeal is always so damn stressful. Every year it's the same thing."

"Well, we got lucky last year, doll. Didn't we just have to leave that once? For a night or two?"

"Yea. We went up to Vicksburg for the night last August for a hurricane. Thankfully, it hit west of us, but I'm so tired of living inside of a bullseye. Going to the Civil War battlefield was cool though."

"Oh yea, there were some really cute guys there."

Realizing that none of those cute guys were

living, or from the last century, she felt it best to change the subject.

"Anyway, I wish we lived in an area without natural disasters, if that sort of place even exists."

"This apartment holds some traumatic memories for me, so I'm not set on staying here. I'm always down for moving when you are ready, but then you'd have to leave Tate without ever getting to be his girl."

Candy pouted cartoonishly, although the thought of Candy's traumatic memories tugged at her heart. Instead of focusing on that, she chose to focus only on the lighter part of the comment.

"Oh hush. I doubt that would ever happen, anyway."

Just as she said it, she secretly hoped she was wrong. She wanted to be Tate's girl, but not at the risk of losing their friendship. Resolving her feelings for him had caused enough of an internal struggle that she had pulled back from him a bit, no longer calling him to spend time with her as she had before. It was agonizing to secretly fall for him, but be unable to do anything about it. Her self-doubt saw to it that she'd never act on her feelings. On a serious note, she thought about how her apartment must have been a tough place for Candy to stay after her death. It was Candy's apartment before she died. It was where her boyfriend, Brad, had killed her. He stabbed her in the back, so she never even saw him coming. Unfortunately, he turned out to be psychotically possessive, and Candy was not right for that kind of man, not that anyone could be. Of all the people she could have had an affair with, the story goes she chose his best friend, Jake. Brad completely lost his mind. She lost her life and he lost his freedom. Candy would still go to the prison, sometimes, and peek in on him, although she spoke little about the man he had become. Hazel never felt comfortable asking her about it. She didn't want to make Candy have to relive anything painful. She realized that Candy's party girl facade, and constant perkiness, was almost certainly armor she had created in order to deal with what she had been through. Hazel didn't want to create any cracks in that armor, not until Candy was ready.

"So, do you think that you're going to get the spirit to speak to you today?" Candy asked.

"I don't know. I don't know what she wants, and this feeling of helplessness is going to eat at me. I need to see her again and at least try. I need to know what she wants from me. I can't just ignore her. She will just keep coming back if I try to ignore her."

Candy patted her on the leg.

"I know and I know you can't ignore her, doll. I just don't want you driving yourself crazy over her if she's not even willing to help herself. There's only so much you can do for them."

Giving Candy's hand a gentle squeeze, she tossed the remote back to her and hopped off of the sofa.

"Shit, my waffles are cold."

"What a shame for such an exquisite cuisine."

"You're on a roll today, mean ass."

"Awe... you know I love you."

Candy turned back to look at the television.

"Love you too, Casper. I've got to go to the prison. See you later."

"Ta ta!" Candy called out while waving over her head.

Hazel stuck one waffle in her mouth, wrapped the other in a napkin before sticking it into her pocket, grabbed her keys and satchel, and headed out of the door.

Traffic was better that morning, since she didn't have to be anywhere near the courthouse until well after 8 a.m., but it was still New Orleans, so there was still congestion on the roads. She chewed on her soggy waffles, washing them down with coffee that was, thankfully, still warm. She was already feeling her headache return, so the sound of the dozen taxi drivers honking their horns on the freeway was not helping her condition at all. Every time she drove in the city, she felt like she was driving on a defensive driving course, or for Nascar, but she couldn't be sure which. Either way, she was always sure she was going to die before she made it to her destination. Pulling up to the jail, she was grateful there were actually parking spots available. Since she arrived at lunchtime, she could park fairly close to the prison. Sweat was still dripping down her back, but she had arrived on time, so she considered that to be a minor victory. If she would have been early enough, she may have even done a victory lap, but a pat to her own back would have to suffice for a job well done.

Hazel didn't have any court appointments that day, so her visit to the prison was her only reason to drive into the downtown traffic. She intended to do the rest of work from home afterwards. That, along with having more laundry to do, was going to make it a super busy day.

Walking into the prison always gave her the creeps, because prisons were usually crawling with spirits. She may have been fairly used to seeing ghosts, since they had been drawn to her since she was a child, but something about knowing she might take a dead criminal home with her was a bit unsettling. The events of the previous twenty-four hours didn't make her feel any better. Two unwelcome spirits showing up in her apartment in one day was not something she would ever be comfortable with. Candy had a good idea about checking into preventative measures, something to try to keep spirits out of her apartment, but she was still on the fence about if she would open a can of worms with using Voodoo methods to do so. Not to mention, she was doubtful anything would actually be effective at keeping them out, but would still allow Candy inside.

Entering the conference room and seeing Roy handcuffed to the table, it was clear she wasn't the only one who hadn't been sleeping. He looked as though he had aged twenty years since she had first met him only recently. Her heart sunk at his appearance. His weight loss, sunken in cheeks, and the shadows under his eyes told her just how miserable he was. She realized she was looking at a haunted man. He had all the signs. Not only was this mysterious spirit's intoxicating energy hard for her to handle, but it was dramatically affecting Roy. If not for herself, she needed to try to pass the spirit on for him, because she wasn't sure how much more exposure his body could handle.

"Roy, you look tired. How are they treating you in here?"

"I mind my business in this place, miss. I've just been having a hard time sleeping and I have nightmares when I do. It's just this place. It's not a place for happiness."

Sounding completely deflated, he covered his mouth and coughed. She slid a cup of water across the table to him. He grabbed it and downed it quickly.

He was not lying. This was not a place of happiness. She knew the constant presence of spirits was draining his energy and making him more exhausted than he would have been otherwise. As usual, his father was by his side, but the mystery woman was not around, or at least she was not showing herself. Hazel needed to speak to her, so she could understand how the spirit was connected to Roy, but she couldn't do that if the spirit wasn't even there. Feeling her stress level rise, she began tapping her finger on the table impatiently. She couldn't just ask Roy if he knew a woman who was about five foot four inches tall, with blond hair and a slender build, who may now be deceased, because she was haunting him. That kind of talk had always made people think she was crazy, and she wanted to try to keep up the facade of normalcy, at least with her clients.

Insistent on getting the interview over with, she attempted to steady her hand and refocus her attention on Roy. She hoped the female spirit would appear, but she couldn't waste the interview in silence while waiting for her.

"Have you received any visitors or contact from your family? I know how lonely you must be. I could try to contact them for you."

"Thank you, Miss Hazel. I called my mom's house yesterday and my auntie told me that my mom's heart is not doing so good. The doctors say she is going to need surgery. My brother, Richard, is coming down from Atlanta to stay with her, and maybe take her back with him so that he can take care of her. I used to take care of my mom before I ended up here, Miss Hazel. I lived with her and my father so that I could take care of them. Now I'm here, and my father is gone, so my mom has lost us both."

He dropped his face into his hands to hide his onset of emotions. His father's spirit moved in closer and placed a hand on his shoulder. He flinched slightly, as though he may have felt it. She wished she could tell him that his father was there, watching over him, but she couldn't. Maybe that would have comforted him, but she couldn't bring herself to do it. She guarded her secret for a reason, and she needed to stick to it.

"I'm so sorry, again, to hear about your father. You and your mother must miss him terribly. Can you tell me a little about him?"

She eyed his father, who was still standing behind him. He smiled at her, nodding in approval.

"Thank you for asking, Miss Hazel. My father was a hardworking man. His name was Reginald. He and my mom had been married for forty-seven years. She was his world. We never had much, but my dad worked hard to give us what we needed. He worked down at the Port of Orleans since he was in his early twenties. A stroke took him from us. My mother was inconsolable. I need to go home to my mom,

Miss Hazel. This heartbreak is killing her. Please help me. I am an innocent man. I shouldn't be here."

The pressure on her shoulders had instantly doubled. She believed he was innocent, but her opinion held no water in the court of law, so she needed actual proof. She needed a minute to speak to his father. She needed the real perpetrator to be caught.

"Can you excuse me for just a moment, Roy?"

"Oh, yes, Miss Hazel," he responded, as he turned to look towards the tiny, barred window on the far wall. There wasn't much sunlight coming in, but it was his only option.

She discreetly motioned to Roy's father to follow her into the hall, hoping he would. Luckily, he did. The guard buzzed the door open for her to leave the conference room and allowed her into the small room next to it. She pretended to be on a telephone call so she could attempt to speak to Mr. Reginald Miller in a secure area without looking like she was talking to herself.

"I'm Hazel, Mr. Reginald. I'm Roy's attorney. I'm trying to help your son."

"I know who you are, Miss Hazel. Thank you for helping my boy. He's a good boy. My Irene needs him right now."

"Is Irene your wife?"

"Yes, ma'am."

"Can you please tell me anything to help me prove Roy's innocence?"

"After I passed, I would spend most of my time with Irene because she had been so sick with her heart. I still spend most of my time with her, but I go back and forth between her and Roy. I make sure to come to Roy when I know you will be with him. I never..."

She interrupted.

"Wait, a minute. How do you know when I'm going to be with Roy so that you can be there as well?"

"People like you are like a flare, Miss Watson, like a fire in the sky. It's like you transmit a signal. When you are in the vicinity, we know where you are."

It was like he was telling her something she

already knew, but didn't want to admit. She couldn't hide from them, even if she wanted to. They would continue to show up unannounced, unless she found a way to keep them out. Even though it felt like something she already knew, hearing it still filled her with dread. She didn't like feeling her life belonged to others, like she couldn't take her life back when helping others became too much for her. She tried to push that feeling aside so she could focus on her conversation with Reginald.

"That explains a lot more than you know. Sorry for interrupting you. Please continue."

"Yes, I was saying that, when I was around Roy while he was at work, I never saw him do anything that appeared inappropriate, not that I know anything about his line of work. I can also vouch to the fact that Roy had no money to show for these so-called riches that he supposedly stole. If he stole all of this money, where did it go? He didn't have that money. His mom and I didn't have that money. None of this makes any sense. He's being used as a scapegoat for someone else. If Roy blames his boss, then I believe him. He's a good man. He's honest. We raised him up right. He needs your help. Let's please go back to him now. He feels incredibly helpless. He needs our support."

"I'll do everything in my power to help him, Mr. Reginald, you have my word."

He gave her a sad smile and then passed between the walls to rejoin his son.

Returning to Roy in the meeting room, she needed to get through with her questioning so she could head home. Something about being there made her chest feel heavy, and the day was already feeling ten times longer than it had been. Not only did Roy insist on his innocence, but so did his father. It was clear, from her interaction with his father, that Roy came from a very close-knit southern family. And in the grand tradition that is the south, his family was dirt poor. The prosecutors claimed that his family's financial woes were his motive for the embezzlement, but she saw his case differently. He was the first person in his family to go to college. He worked very hard to get to where he was. She believed that was reason enough for him to never chance throwing everything he'd worked for away.

Roy looked up at her as she sat back down at the table across from him. She could tell he had been crying. His father had returned to his position behind Roy's back. He had his hand placed on his son's shoulder for support.

"Sorry about that, Roy. And of course I intend to do my best to help you, but it won't be easy. The evidence they are using against you is quite damning. They have documents and emails from your work computer, and paperwork with your signature. I don't know if the documents are authentic, but I need you to be straight with me. Don't leave a single detail out. I need to know the entire story if I'm going to be able to defend you at your trial. These are serious charges. Please start from the beginning. Tell me what you know that led to this."

"I didn't do what they are accusing me of, Miss Watson. My boss, Mr. Raymond Waters, he did that stuff. All of it. He set me up, and the police believed him. Maybe they believed him because

I'm less educated, or poor; I am not sure why, but I am innocent. I swear to you."

"Mr. Miller, I understand. I still need for you to explain to me what happened, what got you into this situation. Can you please try to do that for me? What would Mr. Waters have to gain by framing you? Was he embezzling the money? Do you have reason to suspect that was the case?"

"I can't speak a lot about why Mr. Waters did the things he did. He never did much confiding in me. I was not part of his inner circle. We came from very different worlds. I grew up right here in New Orleans, in the 9th Ward. I was the first person in my family to go to college. I got myself a degree in accounting. I'm not good at a lot of things, Miss Hazel, but math has always been an excellent subject for me. I started working for Mr. Waters about three years ago. I worked for him as an assistant accountant first, but then I got promoted to his lead accountant when my supervisor retired, about a year into my time there. About eight months ago, it seemed like more clients were losing their money on investments. Mr. Waters blamed it on the stock market and the economy. He still wore his usual smile and acted as though things were great, but I could tell he was sometimes angry, especially when I would see him argue with some of the other employees about the finances of the company. I tried to mind my business though, Miss Hazel. I didn't want any trouble. I worked there for a while, but I don't understand everything that is entailed in stock investments, and I don't particularly follow the stock market. I've never had enough money to bother with that stuff. Although many people lost a lot of money, Mr. Waters didn't lose many clients. I'm guessing because his family had been doing business in New Orleans for so long. Mr. Waters is a wealthy and powerful man, and he's a smooth talker. Even if he let people down, he still has a way of making them think he did them a favor. He's slick like that. Then, about four months ago, I overheard Mr. Waters' secretary, Angela Spencer, talking to him about paperwork that was wrong or missing. I didn't hear the entire conversation, and I thought little of it, because our company produces a lot of paperwork. Also, that sort of thing happens often, and if it were something I was supposed to look into, that task would have been delegated to me, so I did not put my nose where it was not welcomed. I never wanted Mr. Waters' anger to be pointed at me. Clearly, this issue with the company's finances needed to go straight to Mr. Waters, and I respected that. By the next day, Angela had quit her job at the firm. Well, that was what Mr. Waters told me. He told us that Angela quit in order to move out of state and take care of her mother, who was ill. I knew there was more to the story than that, but I didn't know her well enough to question what he told me. I heard them having what seemed like a heated conversation, but whether she quit, or he fired her, I'm just not sure. There were rumors in the office that she maybe left because she couldn't deal with Waters anymore, or because he didn't like her snooping behind him. There were even rumors of an affair. I chalked all of that up to workplace gossip. I just don't know the truth. All I know is that Angela left and did not come back."

"So, this woman... Angela... was it? Have you seen or spoken to her since?"

"No, ma'am. I didn't know her outside of work, so I was only told that she moved away."

As he spoke about Angela Spencer, the silent female spirit appeared just over his shoulder. Hazel could at last see more of her face. She had brown eyes and the small creases near her mouth, suggesting that she may have been in her forties. Hazel suspected Angela had possibly died from a blunt force trauma to her head, because she could see a large, bloodied wound on her right side, near the back of her head, but there were also marks around her wrists and ankles. It was possible that the blow to her head, or her sudden death, had affected her ability to comprehend her death, or had prevented her from realizing she could speak to Hazel.

The emotions that bled off of the mysterious spirt were nothing like they had been in days past. Either Hazel had gotten better at blocking the spirit's energy, or the spirit was holding her energy back. She couldn't be sure which, but was grateful for less exposure to it, after all she had experienced during their visit the night before.

The woman gazed down at Roy with the look of sympathy in her eyes. She had on the most beautiful necklace. It was in an art deco design with a large sapphire in the center. Hazel had seen nothing like it before. Within the stone, there appeared to be the shape of a star. The spirit reached up and clutched the necklace with her right hand, rubbing the center sapphire with her thumb. It slightly flickered in and out of visibility as she rubbed it, which took Hazel by surprise. The spirit continued to stare down at Roy, as though trying to send thoughts directly into his mind from hers.

Hazel brought her eyes, nervously, back down to Roy, with a new realization, and it made her feel sick to her stomach. Angela was dead.

"Roy, I will look into Angela and will try to get her side of the story. She may not want to be found, so I cannot make any promises, but I will try. I will get back to you soon."

I have to lie.

She had to lie. Now knowing that Angela was dead, she knew that Angela not wanting to be found wasn't an issue, finding Angela was the issue, but she couldn't reveal that Angela was dead just yet, not until the police knew, or until a body was located. She had to stall.

As she said she would look into Angela, a light seemed to gleam in the spirit's eyes, although Angela never turned her gaze away from Roy. The spirit was Angela. Hazel was almost positive. What she didn't understand was how Angela could be there, in spirit form, yet no one had announced her missing or dead. Something didn't add up and she would have to do some digging. She didn't understand why, if Angela was dead, she was haunting Roy? Did he kill her? He didn't seem the type to do such a thing, but people do horrible things every day. Finding Angela was going to be key in sealing Roy's fate, whether that was bad or good. His case needed a conclusion, but his case had just gotten more complicated. The weight on her shoulders had instantly doubled.

He seemed sad to see her go. She didn't think he had many people to talk to, especially people who would at least consider he did not belong in prison. Roy seemed like a genuine man, but the evidence against him seemed solid. If that didn't give her pause, he was being haunted by a dead woman who used to work with him, however he didn't admit or acknowledge she was dead. That was a troubling conundrum that clouded her mind.

After getting up to walk out of the meeting room where she had sat with Roy, she motioned to Angela, encouraging the wayward spirit to join her in the hallway for a talk, however Angela did not acknowledge Hazel's exit at all. Instead, Angela kept her focus on Roy. By the time Hazel exited the room, Angela was gone. Getting to know what happened to Angela, from Angela, was going to be damn near impossible.

* * *

Before going home, she stopped in at the grocery store so she could grab a few things. Not only were her cabinets and refrigerator bare, but she really needed nonperishable foods, bottled water, and batteries, just in case a severe storm hit New Orleans in the upcoming weeks. She still had both fingers crossed in hopes that the storms would go elsewhere, though. Leaving the grocery store feeling super grown up, as well as $83.47 poorer, she strapped back into her sedan for the fifteen-minute drive home to her apartment.

As soon as she arrived home, she jumped onto her laptop and searched for Angela on social media, but she could not find her on any of the platforms. There were many women with the same name, but none with the same face as the mysterious spirit she believed to be Angela Spencer. Although many people do not use social media, it was one dead end Hazel was hoping not to hit. She knew she was going to have a hard time finding the woman if she had no online presence and there was no missing person report. It really puzzled her why no one seemed to be looking for the missing secretary. Surely, she had family, friends, or someone who loved her, who had noticed her missing?

She pinched the bridge of her nose and closed

her eyes, as though the action would help her think more clearly, but Candy's entrance into the room disturbed her concentration attempt.

"You're looking grumpy today. Do you know what you need? You need a big hunk of some manly lovin. I know a certain cop who could most likely help you with that."

Hazel looked up from her computer screen with her eyes narrowed and arms crossed, feeling entirely unamused, although Candy was wiggling her eyebrows absurdly. Hazel forced herself to keep a straight face.

"What are you up to today, Candy, other than annoying me?"

"Well... I peeked in on the guy who just moved into apartment twelve, and all I've got to say is that I will absolutely visit his dreams tonight!"

Candy was undoubtedly proud of herself.

"Well, I'm sure that will make his week," Hazel noted dismissively, casting her gaze back down to her laptop. Candy, refusing to lose Hazel's attention, moved in closer.

"And you know it, doll." Candy winked.

"Do you even know how to go into his dreams, Candy?"

"Well... no... but I can still pretend... maybe cuddle up on him or something."

Candy shrugged, smiling sheepishly.

"Well, at least one of us will have fun tonight."

"Wait right there! I didn't say that I didn't want to hang out with you tonight. You need to have fun. It's been a while. Let's go out. I need to live vicariously through you! I miss having a real life. Please. Please. Please."

Candy looked up at Hazel and batted her big blue eyes.

"We can't party all day and night, Candy."

Hazel, frustrated, closed the lid of her laptop and returned her eyes to Candy. Candy's face now resembled that of a small child who had just had their toy taken away. She even wore a pout.

"I've just had a long day. You know I met with Roy today. An innocent man is going to go down if I can't do something to stop it, and I am in over my head. Today he told me all of this stuff about how he overheard his boss and the secretary arguing about mishandling money, and that the conversation got heated, and then the secretary never came back to work. He said his boss claims the secretary quit in order to move and take care of her mother. But the lady spirit who I've been seeing, the one who scared the shit out of me last night, well she showed up in the conference room in the prison today, just as he was telling me about the secretary, and there was something about her reaction that told me she is the person who he was talking about. That would mean the secretary almost certainly didn't move away at all, and that she is dead. If she's dead, who killed her? Did Roy kill her, or did his boss do it? I wish she would just give me a damn clue. I've been scouring the web trying to find her, but she appears to have been a hermit. I can't find any social media accounts on her. I'm not sure where to go from here because no one appears to have reported her missing or anything. But one thing that I can say is that this is huge. This is not just a case of embezzlement. This is a case that involves a covered-up murder, and I don't think that the woman's body has even been discovered yet. My mind isn't in the partying mood. I need to figure out what to do next because Angela, the secretary, expects something from me, and I'm not sure what."

"Wow. That is a lot of drama. You need to slow down, doll. You're getting all worked up into a tizzy. You can only do what you can do. Could Roy tell you anything about her at all, other than about the argument?"

"I know. I'm trying. That spirit has been messing with my emotions. I told you basically everything that Roy told me. He spoke like he didn't know her that well. That's why I'm leaning towards thinking he did not commit any of these crimes. I believe his boss is behind all of it. Fine. Let's go out. I need to think about something else for now."

"Yay! I never thought you'd say so! Now, let's find something sexy for you to wear!"

"No way. I'm going like this."

"Hazel, no offense, doll, but you look like a potato... but a cute one. Now change into something cute!"

"Ugh, you're the worst."

"Hey, if you can't be good, then be good at it. That's what I always say,"

Hazel laughed. She'd needed to laugh all day. Compromising, and changing into semi decent street clothes, they headed out the door, hopped into her car, and turned towards downtown.

4

The Missing Woman and the Crush

Candy and Hazel made their way to the French Quarter to check out Candy's favorite bar, but Hazel could not get Angela's face out of her mind. The spirit had been so confused, so desperate. She needed to find out what happened to Angela if she was going to get to the bottom of Roy's case. Her mind raced with theories and scenarios as to what could have happened to the mystery woman. There was going to be no way for her to unwind that night. She let out the deep breath she realized she had been holding. She would have to ruin Candy's plans for the night. She should have known better than to volunteer for a night out. It wasn't like she enjoyed it, even when she didn't have so much on her mind.

"Candy, I've reconsidered. I know you wanted to go to the bar, and you can, but I just can't handle the distraction right now. I'm going to text Tate and see if he might use his policing skills to guide me in the right direction of what to do next in my case. I just don't know how to find out more about Angela with her having no online presence. I don't even know where she lives. Do you hate me?"

"Of course I don't! You know I love you. I understand. And, while you're at it, maybe he can use some other skills, too. You kind of still need that manly lovin."

Candy smirked but Hazel tried to force a scowl.

"Oh, get your mind out of the gutter. This is strictly business."

Hazel tried to hide the flush that was spreading across her cheeks. She didn't know why she bothered to hide it from Candy, because Candy always knew how she felt about Tate.

"Alright. Alright."

Candy waved her hand in surrender.

"I'm your ride or die, doll. I'll stay with you tonight. Plus, that Tate is quite a snack. I wouldn't mind the view."

Candy flashed her a gleaming smile but her scowl deepened.

Feeling a bit relieved, Hazel pulled over onto the shoulder of the road, sent a text to Tate, and made a U-turn to head back in the opposite direction. He agreed to meet up with her at City Park, which was several miles away. She and Candy headed that way instantly. A bit of excitement always shot through her when she got to see him, and that night was no different, even if it wasn't for a social call.

Sitting in City Park at night in New Orleans was unnerving. Throughout her time in New

Orleans, she had seen occupied body bags strewn along sidewalks as people went along their way, in and out of nightclubs, as though the body was not there. She had also witnessed groups of men beat individuals to a bloody pulp in the middle of the street during rush hour traffic. That was New Orleans violence. It was a part of life here. People seemed almost desensitized to it. She sat in her car with the doors locked and waited for him to arrive. Thankfully, he didn't keep her waiting for very long. Just before she lost her nerve from being a sitting duck, his cruiser pulled up beside her car. He hopped out of his police car and jumped into hers with a jubilant plop.

Tate, a college friend of hers, was a deputy with the New Orleans Police Department. He towered over Hazel, at six feet tall, which was a mountain to her 5-foot three-inch frame. His broad shoulders qualified all of his hugs as bear hugs, and she accepted them any time he offered. They had shared a few classes during their freshmen year, and he had asked her for dates ever since. She had never taken it seriously. Hazel, the habitual non-dater, had never agreed, more because of her fear of losing him as a friend, than because of a lack of attraction to him. Also plagued with low self-esteem, she had never felt good enough for him. Surely his flirtation with her was all in good fun and not the real deal, or at least that was what she told herself. Instead of putting herself out there, and trying to get what she wanted, she continued to completely fawn over him in silence, and torture herself. They had always remained great friends, though.

Tate was a great guy and had always been willing to entertain her when she needed a bit of information he could provide. However, she never divulged the secret to him about her ability to see spirits because she didn't want him to think she was crazy. Telling someone she could see spirits didn't always have a favorable outcome. Many times, it had caused her to get doors slammed in her face or phones hung up on her. She didn't want that to happen between her and Tate. She wanted to trust him to understand, but she didn't want to bet their friendship on it.

"Hey girl, want a date?"

Tate smiled at her playfully, still partially hanging out of her car.

"You're silly. Close door before we get robbed."

"You're safe with me."

He beamed and his smile nearly melted her heart.

As he closed the car door, she could see his muscles flex, causing a warm flush to flood throughout her body. She tried to play it off, but she wasn't sure if the attempt was successful. Glancing in the rearview mirror, she could tell, by Candy's facial expression, that she had failed miserably. She was about as smooth as sandpaper and she knew it. That realization only made her flush more. Candy, sitting in the backseat, pretending to make out with an invisible person, only made it harder for Hazel to keep her composure. She threw a threatening look to Candy, before turning her eyes back to Tate.

"Thank you for coming. I actually texted you because I have a bit of a mystery on my hands."

Plus she really wanted to see him, although she didn't dare say it out loud.

"I'm intrigued. Go on."

He looked at her curiously, leaning in close enough for her to smell his cologne. She explained her conversation with Roy, while Tate listened attentively, nodding periodically in acknowledgment. She told him she needed to question Angela about the paperwork debacle at Roy's workplace, but she didn't tell him that Angela was already dead. Tate didn't know about her abilities and she wasn't ready to disclose the truth to him yet. Just the thought of it made her stomach swirl. She resigned to the idea that she may have to find Angela's body herself, or hope the police beat her to it, but she had no way to tell the police that Angela was dead without explaining how she knew, while they didn't. Tate went into his work computer, found Angela's last known address, and wrote it down for her.

"Thank you. I'll let you know what I find out. Oh, can you do one more favor for me?"

She smiled at him sheepishly. He arched one eyebrow, which secretly drove her a bit crazy, but in a good way.

"Maybe... depends on what it is."

She pulled the parking ticket out of her bag and unfolded it, setting it onto the dash board. Tate looked amused, slightly covering his mouth as he chuckled.

"Could you...," she murmured, before trailing off and looking down towards the floorboard. She felt quite embarrassed, and she knew she was doing a terrible job at hiding it.

"I can try, but you have to try to stop collecting these," he teased, but he took the ticket and placed it in his pocket. "Alright, girl, now get home safe. I'll get back to you on the ticket."

He hopped out of her sedan, but unexpectedly popped his head back in.

"Oh, and Hazel..."

"Yea?"

"How about you call me sometimes, just to hangout, huh? It's been a while."

"Oh, okay, yea, that sounds great."

"In that case, see you real soon."

"Okay, bye, Tate."

He turned away and walked back to his police cruiser. Her heart fluttered. She couldn't help but watch him walk away, like a babbling schoolgirl, until Candy disturbed the moment.

"Tate and Hazel sitting in a tree, K-I-S-S-I."

"OH, SHUT UP!"

Candy laughed

"Oh, all right."

Hazel waited for him to leave before she backed out. Truth was that, although he told her to get home safely, she wasn't going home. She was going to take her chances and go to Angela's last known address. Hopefully, someone who knew Angela still lived there and could at least point her in the right direction where Angela could have gone, or at least who she could have gone with.

Driving over, she did not know what she was getting into. She didn't know who lived at the house, or if anyone even did. For all she knew, Angela's killer could have inhabited it. It was a risk for her to go there at all. Her racing heart told her that. Not even having a story prepared for why she was going there, she knew she would have to come up with it all on the fly.

"Are you ready for this? You know, we don't have to go tonight. We can always wait until it's daytime," Candy suggested.

"No, we're already almost there. Plus, I don't think I'd ever be ready. We will just stop really quick and see if she still lives there. We don't even know if anyone lives there anymore."

Her heart rate increased as she pulled down the street to her destination.

Getting out of her car, there were so many thoughts going through her head, many of which were reasons for her to turn around and go back home, but she put all of her doubts in the back of her mind and walked towards the front door. She felt like she had no choice. As she got close to the front stoop, Angela materialized in front of her, blocking her path. Hazel assumed that Angela's upheld arms meant she was ready to speak to her, but when she got up close to her, she ended up walking right through her. Angela had vanished. Hazel felt the hair stand up on the back of her neck and she spun around frantically, trying to figure out where the spirit had gone.

"Did you see that? Did you see where she went?"

Hazel turned to Candy, feeling exasperated.

"No way to know, doll. She dematerialized. There's no way to know where she went unless she appears again. You know," Candy hesitated, "she may not be disappearing on purpose. Her spirit may just be too weak to control her manifestations."

"You're probably right."

"But did you see what she was doing?"

Candy looked concerned, slightly blocking Hazel's path to the front door.

"What do you mean?"

"I think she was trying to tell you to turn back. Maybe we should go home. Maybe it's not safe."

"I'm already here, and I've got you. Also, Tate gave me this address, so he knows to look here for me if anything happens. I think it'll be okay. We will be quick. This isn't where Raymond

Waters lives, and I'm pretty sure he is her killer, anyway."

"Yea, but you don't know for sure, Hazel."

Hazel, already ignoring the last point, had knocked on the door. A man opened the door but left the chain lock in place to where she could only see part of his face. The smell of cheap whiskey met her face before his eyes did. His hairline had receded and, from the look of the bags under his eyes, so had his bedtime. He was not a man who prioritized sleep. He was possibly in his mid-forties, but a hard life made him look much older. She could hear a late-night pundit blaring from a tv in the background. It was one of those television programs that was more propaganda than news.

"Can I help you?" he asked with a strong Cajun accent.

"I'm sorry for showing up so late. My name is Hazel Watson and I'm an attorney with the public defender's office. I'm representing a man who used to work with Angela Spencer, and I was given this as her last known address. Is she here?"

"No, ma'am, I'm sorry. Angela no longer lives here. I'm John. She is my ex-wife. She moved out of here about five months ago."

Hazel felt a glimmer of hope fizzle out. She shifted her weight nervously as she began feeling uncomfortable. She wasn't one to stand on the strange man's porch in the middle of the night. Candy saw the change in her posture and moved in closer for support.

"Do you still speak to her? Do you know where she currently lives?"

"I'm sorry, ma'am, but what is this all about? I haven't spoken to Angela in a few months. Is she in some kind of trouble?"

He appeared slightly suspicious of her. He eyed her wearily.

"Maybe. She may be missing. After speaking to my client, the man who used to work with Angela, it sounds like Angela either left town, or disappeared. I'm trying to find out which. Do you have her mother's contact information or address?"

"Missing? There's no way. What do you mean? Please come in while I try to call her."

John unlocked the chain latch and allowed her into his small home. Her survival instinct screamed, but she entered anyway. He grabbed the remote control and shut the television off, to her delight, while grabbing his cell off of the kitchen counter. He motioned to the table for her to take a seat while he dialed numbers on his phone. She looked around from the table as John paced. He was obviously troubled. She didn't get the feeling he had anything to do with Angela's disappearance, not that she knew him at all. It was clear from his home he was a single, blue-collared man. He had perhaps been drowning his sorrows in the bottle every day after work ever since his separation. She saw that he still kept an old picture of him and Angela on the wall, both smiling while holding fishing poles. This man had not moved on.

After a few failed phone calls, John set his phone down and sat at the table across from her. He lowered his brow, rubbing his eyes with his hands, and then he glanced around the room, refusing to make eye contact with her for a few awkward moments. She could tell he was feeling nervous. When she felt desperately uncomfortable from the silence, he pulled over an ashtray and lit a cigarette. She turned her body to the side, trying to distance herself from the assaulting smoke.

She waited a moment before breaking the silence, but he spoke before she had to.

"She didn't answer, and that isn't like her. I called her cell and her apartment and received no answer on either phone. The voicemail boxes on both were full, so she hasn't been checking them. I told you before that Angela and I talk very little, but this is not like her. I would like to ride by her apartment and check it out."

"I'll go ride with you. Maybe I would pick up on something you miss."

Candy made a face, suggesting that was a bad idea, but Hazel was undeterred. Even with Candy's objection, she was glad for the lead. Before that moment, she hadn't even known Angela had an apartment. Seeing Angela's apartment would help her rule out that location as being where Angela's body was, or at least being the location of where she was murdered. If they had found her there, or found any evidence, they would obviously call the police, but they needed to at least rule it out.

John tried to grab for his car keys, but having had drinks before she arrived, she offered to drive instead. He willingly allowed her the concession. Grabbing his hat and house keys, he opened the door and they walked outside together. Candy objected all the way to the car but Hazel felt she had no choice but to take a look in Angela's apartment. John seemed to be her only way to do that, since she didn't even know where the apartment was, so she had to go with him, even if she didn't feel comfortable doing it.

The drive to Angela's apartment was quiet, awkward, but brief. Being so late at night, there wasn't much traffic, and Angela didn't live that far away from the home she had once shared with John. Hazel consciously had to fight back the uneasiness she felt from having a strange man in her car. At the house, it seemed like a great idea to ride with him to Angela's apartment, but hindsight felt differently. At least she had Candy with her. Having Candy there was the one thing that kept her grounded.

The complex was rather small, with only a few units next to a bakery. It looked like the most Angela might have been able to afford on an individual salary in New Orleans. They got to Angela's door and John opened it with a spare key. She was a bit taken aback that he had a key, but he explained Angela had given it to him since he was the only person she knew in the city in case there was an emergency. The story seemed to make enough sense, and it was an actual emergency, so she shrugged it off.

They walked into the apartment and realized no one else had been there in weeks. The air was stale. There were still dishes in the sink and food in the refrigerator. She still had laundry on her bed. Angela had not left for good. She fully intended to come home. She just never had the chance.

Hazel felt that she still needed to visit Angela's mother, but she was less confident she would find the solution to Angela's disappearance there.

She and John had driven back to his home in the same relative silence they had driven to Angela's apartment in, although she was less worried that he was going to kill her. The mood felt very somber. She could tell he felt hopeless, but he still went inside to get Angela's mother's information for her, just in case it wasn't a lost cause.

He came back armed with a slip of paper with a Mobile, Alabama, address and telephone number on it, which meant she would need to take an out-of-town trip in order to speak with Angela's mother. If Angela's mother knew where she had gone, Hazel intended to find out.

She and Candy stopped at the apartment, packed a small bag, and then headed out for the two-hour drive to Mobile. It was too late to show up on an elderly woman's doorstep, so they reserved a hotel room and planned to go to see Angela's mother first thing the next morning.

* * *

They didn't get to the hotel until really late. Candy had, thankfully, kept her entertained by talking during the entire drive. She mostly rambled on about boys, well, mainly one boy, Tate. Hazel's heart always fluttered, just a little, when thinking about him, so there were definitely worse things they could've talked about for two hours. Candy always had so much to say, but Hazel didn't really mind. She wasn't as much of a talker, so it was better than hours of awkward silences, which is what she usually contributed to conversations, although she was better at filling the space when talking to Candy. By the time they had gotten to the hotel, her mood had shifted, and she was dreading the nightmares that waited for her. After such a long day, she fell asleep as soon as her head hit the pillow, but her sleep was fitful.

Her dreams hit her with the violence of a freight train, nearly startling her awake, and plaguing her throughout the entire night.

* * *

Unable to hold back tears, I struggled against the cloth in my mouth. I could taste the day old sweat that permeated it, and feel the crisscross pattern of the fabric on my tongue. Using my tongue as a wedge, I tried to push the cloth off of my mouth, but it was tied too tightly. The vehicle bounced forcefully, causing me to bang my head against the roof of the trunk. Shrieking from the impact, I could no longer hold back tears as my head throbbed. I tried to kick against the back of the taillights, but my bound feet gave me no freedom to do so. I felt helpless and alone. There was nothing I could do to get myself out of there, and I feared what would happen to me at the end of the drive. As the car slowed to a stop, my heart rate rose, and I began to hyperventilate, causing me to get lightheaded. When the trunk opened, it was dark out, so all I could see were the trees that were illuminated in the glow of the taillights. I saw no-one, other than him. The sight of him made my heart fall, like a weight, into my feet. Feeling a rush of energy, I tried to scream, intending to fight back, but before I had the chance, I felt a flare of pain in the back of my head, which caused the world to spin. The spiral it created sucked me further down into the blackness and I was unable to claw myself out.

* * *

Hazel's eyes opened, hoping the sun would not be shining through the curtains of the hotel window, only to be disappointed that it was.

Even on days when she could afford to sleep in, her body had other plans. Between the late night of driving, after meeting with Tate, John, and going to Angela's abandoned apartment, she most likely had only gotten a few hours of genuine sleep. She felt like she was falling into critical levels of dysfunction.

She rubbed the sleep out of her eyes as she watched Candy float across the room to join her.

"I'm getting worried about you, doll. You were thrashing in your sleep last night. I don't know how you will continue to function if this keeps happening to you. Maybe you should see someone about the nightmares?"

"Thank you for looking out for me, Candy. I don't know why my nightmares have gotten so much more intense these days. I'm thinking that they are not nightmares, and that they are in fact memories, maybe they are Angela's memories. Maybe she is trying to show me what happened to her. I dreamed I was bound and gagged. I was in the trunk of a car, like I had been in other dreams. It was too dark to see features but I know I was brought to a heavily treed area by a man. I was terrified and panicking. I still feel a bit uneasy from it."

Candy sat next to her on the bed, placing a hand on her shoulder. The chill from Candy's icy hand traveled from her shoulder, all the way through her body. She pulled the blankets tighter around herself to compensate. Candy's energy calmed her, no matter how cold it was to be near her.

"Oh my. That sounds terrifying. You poor thing. That would certainly explain it. I wonder why she would choose to show you these images in your dreams instead of just coming and speaking to you? She's not doing herself any favors if she wants her body to be found, or if she wants justice for herself or Roy. It's like she's torturing you."

"That's the same thing that I don't understand. Maybe she is confused and doesn't know that she can speak to me, or maybe she doesn't know that she is dead. Perhaps her energy is forcing these images onto me, without her direct knowledge. The entire thing is a puzzle to me. Hopefully, she eventually comes around. Until then, I will just keep trying to see what more I can find out on my own."

"I understand why you're doing it, but I wish she would stop tormenting you, and just communicate with you directly."

Candy gently wrapped her arm around Hazel's shoulders.

"As do I, but I don't know if it's in her control. Thank you, again, for looking out for me, but we have to get going."

Hazel climbed off of the bed and began getting ready to leave the hotel.

Grabbing a biscuit and coffee from the hotel lobby, as they walked to her car, they headed on their way to the home of Angela's mother. Hazel knew she would need to create a cover story as to why she was asking so many questions about Angela's whereabouts, but she hadn't come up with one yet. She couldn't even pretend to know how Angela's family would react to a stranger coming to their door and raising alarms, because she didn't know anything about them at all. With any luck, Angela's family would buy her story and would give her information that would get her closer to finding out what happened to the missing woman. If she could leave with them agreeing to file a missing person's report, that would be considered a win.

Downtown Mobile reminded her a lot of the Garden District in New Orleans. Its tree-lined streets had old growth oaks that folded over the roads and encircled it like an all-natural tunnel. Being such an old city, scattered Greek revival homes, that had been built in the mid-1800s, stood out like something from an old painting. Trendy little shops and cafes lined the streets. People in business attire, and others out shopping, shuffled along the sidewalks. She imagined returning for a visit one day, maybe when the weather was less steamy.

They arrived at the address John had given to her at 11:15 a.m. It was a quaint little house on the outskirts of Mobile. It looked to have been built around the 1960s. It reminded her of a house that you would see on a 60s sitcom with a four-piece family and a stay-at-home mother, dog included. It was painted in pastel colors with a white picket fence. It could not have gotten more traditional. She could tell a lot of pride had gone into the house, however, assuming because of Angela's mother's illness, the landscaping had been neglected. Although the grass appeared to have been recently trimmed, the flower beds had sprouted enough weeds to be considered a hostile takeover.

As she approached the front porch, she could see an elderly man looking out of an upstairs window. She waved up at him and smiled, but he backed away from the window. The curtain closed in front of him, blocking her view.

"That was kind of rude," Candy scoffed, in response to the man in the window. "He could've at least waved back. Old grump."

"Yea, that was kind of weird."

Hazel felt uncomfortable, but she finished walking to the front door.

She knocked on the front door and a woman with a thick Spanish accent answered. Hazel realized, right away, that the woman could not have been Angela's mother. She only appeared to be in her fifties, so she was definitely too young to have a daughter in her mid-forties. Off in the background, she could see an elderly woman in a wheelchair. The elderly woman was gazing out of the window and did not acknowledge her visitor's presence. She did not see the elderly man downstairs at all.

Maybe he doesn't like unexpected guests like the rest of us. Awesome.

"Can I help you, mija?" the lady asked politely. She was wearing a purple pair of scrubs, with her hair in a bun.

"Yes, ma'am. I'm looking for Ms. Harriet Wilson. I'm a friend of Angela's and was told that I may find her here."

"I'm sorry, miss. This is Ms. Harriet's home. I'm her home health nurse, Sylvia, but Mrs. Angela hasn't been here since Christmas. Who did you say that you were?"

"My name is Hazel Watson. I'm a friend of Angela's from New Orleans. She left a few months ago and I haven't seen her since. She also isn't answering either of her phones or checking her voicemails. I was worried, so I thought that her mother may know of her whereabouts."

"I'm afraid that Ms. Harriet doesn't know much these days. She has dementia. It's only been getting worse. I don't think it will be long before she is no longer with us. I think she is waiting to see Angela again before she lets go, but it is just the two of us here. I am not sure where Mrs. Angela would be. I have not spoken to her either."

"Only the two of them here?" Candy whispered into her ear. "I guess we are with another ghost. I'll go have a chat with him and see what I can find out."

"Would you like to come in, dear? I can put on a pot of coffee."

"Thank you, Sylvia. I can stay for a bit. I appreciate it."

As Sylvia walked into the kitchen to brew the coffee, Hazel could see that Harriet was not only looking out of the window, but also appeared to be mumbling to herself. Hazel was drawn over to the back wall of the living area where there were dozens of pictures on the walls and shelves. Several were of Angela. She appeared in her sapphire necklace often, specifically in her later years. It must have been special to her.

She walked closer to Mrs. Harriet and lowered herself to the elderly woman's level. She wanted to see if she could make out what Harriet was murmuring. Most of it sounded like gibberish. She could only make out a few words. It sounded like she was saying tree, Angela, help, bring her home. There was desperation in the old woman's voice that made Hazel's heart ache, but she didn't know how to help her. All she thought she could do was try to find Angela for her. Maybe that would bring both women peace. She knelt there for a moment, and placed her hand affectionately onto Mrs. Harriet's hand, which rested on top of her lap. She wanted Mrs. Harriet to know that she wasn't alone. Suddenly, the elderly women jerked her head around to face Hazel and squeezed Hazel's hand so hard that it sent a shock of pain up her arm. Hazel stood there, in complete and utter horror, while Mrs. Harriet repeated her mumbling chant louder, straight to Hazel's face: "TREE, ANGELA, HELP, BRING HER HOME."

Tears streamed out of Hazel's eyes as she tried to pry her hand loose, but Harriet would not let her go. Instead, Harriet squeezed her hand tighter the more Hazel tried to free herself.

After several long moments, through struggled sobs, Hazel cried: "I will, I will bring her home."

Something clicked in Harriet, after Hazel promised to bring Angela home, causing a quick transition in her behavior. Harriet let go of Hazel's hand, returned her lifeless gaze to the window, and began her senseless mumble again. Hazel lifted herself back onto straightened legs, safely moving a few steps away. She stood there for a few moments, suspended in disbelief, unsure of what had just happened.

As she was trying to gather her thoughts, she glimpsed a figure moving in the corner of her eye, walking into a back bedroom. Feeling the need to follow it, she asked Sylvia for directions to the bathroom before following the spirit into the back of the house. Down the hall, and into the bedroom to the right, she entered the bedroom and saw Angela. Angela was kneeling on the floor near the edge of the bed, trying to open a wooden trunk that was tucked just beneath the foot board. Although she appeared to be unable to open the trunk, she continued to struggle against its metal latch.

"Angela," Hazel gently called out, "please don't leave. I need to talk to you."

Angela fiddled with the latch only a few moments longer, oblivious to Hazel's presence, but when she looked up and noticed her in the doorway, Angela vanished.

Just as Angela vanished, Candy appeared in the doorway, standing right next to Hazel.

"What happened? Why are you in this room?"

Candy caught sight of the same trunk Hazel was eyeing.

"I followed Angela in here. She disappeared right before you showed up."

"Damn. What is it with her and her magic tricks?"

"I really don't think she has accepted that she is dead yet. Her spirit wasn't strong enough to open this trunk, but she tried. She isn't strong like you. Maybe that is why she won't speak to me. Maybe she doesn't even know that she can."

"Hmm... have you looked into the trunk yet?"

Candy eyed the trunk as though it held hidden treasures.

"Not yet. I was thinking about it right before you walked in."

"Well, get on with it then."

Candy knelt down in front of the trunk, motioning to Hazel to join her. Hazel walked over to the trunk and opened it. Inside, she found stacks of documents, all appearing to be from Waters' Financial Firm. Both her and Candy's mouths dropped. She felt excitement flood through her body, almost like a new avenue to win Roy's case had burst open.

"Maybe she was trying to get these documents because they could help Roy," Hazel suggested, while flipping through the paperwork.

"This is a significant find, Hazel. This should really help your case."

"Yea..."

The mountain of paperwork included bank statements, check records, printed emails, and other various financial documents. She quickly stuck the stack of papers into her satchel and then closed the trunk, quietly tucking it back under the bed. For whatever reason, Angela wanted these documents. Hazel needed to take them. She needed to find out what was so important in them that Angela would take time out of her afterlife to get to them.

"Did you speak to the old man upstairs?"

"Of course, I did, honey. You know that gossip is my specialty."

"So, what did he say?"

"Well, his name is Earl, and he is Harriet's husband and Angela's father. He said he had a heart attack about two years ago."

"If he had a heart attack two years ago, why is he still here? He should have crossed over by now."

"He is here to guide his wife on. He said that it won't be long. The only problem is she won't pass on until she sees Angela again, but she doesn't know that Angela has passed away. Earl tries to encourage Harriet to pass on, and to make her understand she will see Angela again, but Harriet doesn't understand because of her dementia. He's waiting for her body to give out."

"Wow, that's so sad. So, I don't need to cross over only one spirit. I will need to help three. This just got much more complicated. I'm going to talk with Sylvia a bit to see what I can find out. Maybe I can get them to file a missing person's case. With Angela not speaking to me, or helping me to help her, I may need the police in on this after all."

"That would be the safer route, Hazel. I don't like you working on murder cases by yourself. I don't want you to end up like me."

"I'll be okay. I've got you. I'm rarely by myself anymore."

Hazel flashed Candy an assuring smile, although she didn't feel as confident as she led on.

As she walked back into the kitchen, she ran through how she could approach the conversation so she could get information without setting off any alarm bells, but she decided that at least the partial truth was best. Pushing her self-doubts aside, she took her chances of raising the alarm about Angela's disappearance. Honesty was the best policy, and she didn't want this to come back to bite her when Angela's body was finally found. She would just leave out the part about the spirits. She finally made her way to the kitchen to find that Sylvia was busying herself with a plate of pastries. It relieved her to think Sylvia may have not even noticed her wander off.

She pulled out a chair and sat at the table, signaling her return to Sylvia, who shuffled over with two coffee cups and the plate of pastries.

"Here you go, mija. The coffee is hot, so be careful," Sylvia said.

"Thank you, Ms. Sylvia, but you didn't have to go through so much trouble."

"It's no trouble at all! We don't get many visitors. I'm here with Mrs. Harriet every day, and she, sadly, no longer talks to me, so it gets quite lonely. Tell me more about what brings you all this way."

Blowing on her hot coffee, Hazel swallowed back her nervousness and began her explanation.

"Sylvia, I'm here because I'm really worried about Angela. No one seems to have seen her in quite a while. I'm afraid that something bad has happened to her. I met with her ex-husband, John, last night. He hasn't seen her in a few months, either. We checked her phones and her apartment. There seems to be no trace of her. She left work and has disappeared. Do you have any ideas where she could be?"

There was a long pause. Sylvia looked troubled. The pleasant look that had been on her face when they sat down had turned cloudy. Hazel could see that Sylvia was thinking hard about something but was perhaps unsure if she should bring it up.

Finally, Sylvia broke the silence.

"I don't know of anyone who could have ill will against Ms. Angela or could hurt her except."

She trailed off. Sylvia looked towards the living room and seemed to lose focus.

"Except what? I'm sorry for being pushy, but I am afraid that Angela is in danger. Any information could help her. If you know anything that could help, please tell me."

Whatever she said had seemed to cause Sylvia to pause.

"I said 'except' because, when Angela divorced John, they didn't end on the best terms," she hesitated. "Mrs. Angela is a kind woman with a lot of integrity. I can't think of anyone who would want to harm her, but I know she and John had a rather toxic marriage. If you're looking for someone who may have ill will against her, I'd look into him," she explained.

Hazel felt uneasiness rise within her. Had she read John wrong? Had she unknowingly spent time alone with a man who was capable of murder? The thoughts threatened to take over in her head space, but she quickly pulled herself back into the conversation.

"Had he ever hurt Angela? Physically, I mean?"

Sylvia took a moment to ponder the question.

"I'm not sure. She never told me anything. I, unfortunately, did witness many of their arguments. John was a drinker, and I believe it got worse throughout their relationship. Angela used to come here, sometimes, just to get away from him," she responded.

"Wow... That's awful. It makes me feel uneasy about having spent time with him now, but he seemed truly concerned for her when I spoke to him. I don't claim to know what went on in their marriage, but I did not get the feeling that he had anything to do with her disappearance, but I'm obviously not a detective or anything. No matter what, she seems to be missing, so we need to involve the police in the search. I hoped you could help to get that started."

Sylvia nodded in acknowledgement.

"Yes, I will contact the police station and file a missing person's report. Leave your phone number with me and I'll call you with any updates."

"That would help a lot, Sylvia. Thank you so much. I will contact you with any updates as well."

She gave her contact information to Sylvia and then she and Candy left the house.

With any luck, the missing person's report

would lead to Angela being found, and it would bring the guilty party to justice. Meanwhile, she had all the paperwork she had taken from Angela's bedroom to go through. There was obviously a reason Angela had kept it hidden in that trunk. Maybe it held evidence that she had on Raymond Waters, proof he was the one embezzling money from his own company, not Roy. She needed to find out why Angela kept those documents, and she still needed to find out how Roy fit into all of it.

She felt a sense of relief on the drive home from Mobile, but only slightly. Getting the police involved in the search for Angela's body would help to take some of the burden off of her, but it would also cause her to be involved in a police investigation, one that she strictly wasn't supposed to be involved in. That fact made her very uncomfortable. She didn't want to get into any trouble with the police, so she would have to trod more carefully. Knowing she tread about as carefully as a hippopotamus in an antiques shop, all she could do was sigh.

5

The Truth
and the
Stone

Darkness. All I see is darkness. I hear the swarming cicadas. I smell the sticky mud as my feet sink down into the marsh. I feel a tightness in my chest as my cortisol level rises, causing my breath to come in short bursts. Having no one to fight, I feel the need to run, but there doesn't appear to be anywhere to run to. I glance around, but I see no one. The darkness is too

thick, almost as though I am deep within a void, and only sounds and smells can make it through. I try to remember how I ended up here, but my mind only came back empty. I couldn't remember anything. I shiver as it begins to rain, but the rain is light, as its drops scatter across my face. The coolness of it feels good against my skin, but something feels wrong. It's the only thing telling me that I might still be alive.

* * *

Hazel woke up suddenly to the sound of her own heartbeat, from what she believed to be another memory. This memory, like the others, was not hers, but it made her feel like she had lived through the experience. Lightheaded, because of her rapid breathing, she was taken aback from the realness of the experience. She had felt like she was somewhere in the swamps, but she must have been blindfolded, because she couldn't see her surroundings. She could smell it, however. She could even hear it. The smells and sounds still filled her senses. They haunted her. She wrapped her arms around her body and rubbed the chill out of her arms. The dream had made her feel trapped, a feeling she hadn't been able to shake immediately upon waking up. She felt a sudden sense of dread realizing that Angela's last moments would have felt like that. She would have felt cold and alone, her feet sinking into the mud while rain came down upon her. She must have been terrified. With the endless swamps in the state of Louisiana, and its bone crushing alligators, she shuttered to think of what could have become of her. Imagining Angela's final moments only caused Hazel to feel all the more traumatized by witnessing it through her dreams. She still had no idea how Angela was pushing memories into her head, but Hazel no longer had the ability to push them from her mind. Even once Angela had crossed through the veil, over to the other side, there was no way to send her memories with her. Hazel frowned, realizing she may have to relive Angela's memories for the rest of her life, although they weren't her memories at all. She felt overwhelmed by them, and she couldn't imagine how she would be able to forget them, unless she tried therapy, and she wasn't even convinced therapy would work.

She jumped into the shower, hoping the warm water would help her shake the feeling that had come over her. Having an appointment with Roy meant she couldn't spend the day dwelling over what she had experienced. She had no choice but to move on with her day.

"Good morning!"

Candy poked her head in through the shower curtain, nearly making Hazel fall on her face. She instinctively tried to cover her nakedness, unsuccessfully.

"Candy!" Hazel shrieked. "Are you trying to kill me? You scared the shit out of me. Couldn't you wait until I got out of the shower?"

"Awe, but I missed you. Why are you bothering trying to cover yourself?"

Candy smirked as she motioned to the tiny towel that was barely covering Hazel's chest.

"Don't be silly. Mine are bigger anyway."

Candy smiled, but Hazel could think of nothing else to do but stick out her tongue, like a normal adult.

"Can you at least back your head out of the shower and talk to me?"

Hazel flicked her hand in the direction she wanted Candy to go. Candy obliged, dramatically backing her head out of the shower, making Hazel break out into laughter. Candy's exit from the shower looked really unnatural, as though she was being rolled out on wheels. Once Candy's head was fully outside of the shower, she dared to continue their conversation.

"So... what are you up to today?"

"I have to go to the prison and meet with Roy. I need to get a better understanding of his relationship with Angela, but I had this really freaky nightmare last night, so I may have a hard time doing my job today... feeling like I just narrowly escaped abduction and all..."

"That just doesn't sound right, love. I wish there was something that you could do about those nightmares, or memories, whatever they are. Repeatedly having experiences like that, on top of the lack of sleep, can't be good for your physical or mental health."

"Yea, I know, but I don't know how to make them stop coming to me."

She got out of the shower, but was forced to steady herself on the sink due to a brief onset of dizziness, possibly caused by the memory of her nightmare. Candy reached out to help her but the feeling passed almost as quickly as it came on.

"Do you think the nightmare was one of Angela's memories again?"

"Definitely. It had a lot in common with others that I've had in the past."

"Well, I hope you can put her behind you soon. She's having a real negative impact on your life, much more than other spirits you've helped in the past."

"I know. Thanks for the talk, Candy, but I've got to get going."

Returning to her bedroom, Hazel put on a pair of gray slacks with a black blouse. She threw her hair into a ponytail and headed towards the door.

* * *

Hazel got to the prison at about 9 a.m., after taking a moment to go through a fast food drive thru for breakfast. Walking into the conference room where Roy was shackled to the table was an unsettling sight. She had seen him cuffed and shackled before, but it never got easier to see an innocent man being chained up a notch above the treatment of an animal. His face looked gaunt. She could tell that he still wasn't sleeping. The worst part was she knew he didn't even belong in prison at all. An innocent man's future hung on her shoulders, and she didn't know if she could pull off what needed to happen in order to set him free. The weight was bearing down on her, and it was crushing.

Putting her feelings aside, she faked a smile for Roy's sake and sat down across from him.

"Good morning, Roy. I brought you some fresh coffee and a breakfast sandwich. You look like you could use it. How are you feeling?"

She slid a black coffee and breakfast sandwich across the table to the broken man on the other side. His eyes had a glint of a sparkle as he grabbed his food and coffee. He opened the lid on his coffee and took a satisfying first sip. Hopefully, the gesture would give him the small boost he needed to get him through the day. She wished she could have done more.

"I'm just tired, Miss Hazel. Thank you so much for bringing me breakfast this morning. It's hard for me to eat here. The food isn't like what my mom used to make. I'm still having a lot of trouble sleeping and I'm feeling really stressed. I hope that you have some good news for me. I don't belong here, Miss Hazel. I need to be with my mom."

"I do have some interesting information to share with you, Mr. Miller. I did some digging into Mrs. Angela Spencer. I went to her previous address and spoke to her ex-husband. He didn't know where she was. He said he hadn't heard from her in a long time. He gave her mother's address to me, so I took a trip to visit with her in Mobile, Alabama, and Angela was not there. Mr. Waters lied to you about Angela moving to be with her mother. Her mother has dementia, so I wasn't able to speak with her directly, however her mother's home health nurse confirmed that Angela had not been back to Mobile since Christmas. The nurse is filing a missing person's report. Angela's ex-husband and I also took a ride to her apartment, which appeared to have been abandoned. She is missing, Roy. If you know anything more about her disappearance, I need for you to tell me now. No detail is too small. Figuring out what happened to her could be the key to proving your innocence."

By the time Hazel finished talking, Roy's eyes were wide, but his face was blank. He didn't speak for a while, but she gave him the time he needed. He still hadn't eaten any of his sandwich. She hoped stress wouldn't prevent him from eventually enjoying it. He finally rubbed his hands down the front of his face and then fixed his eyes on her.

"Are you telling me she is gone? Like something bad happened to her?"

Roy was unable to hide the disbelief in his voice. His eyes had grown big enough for Hazel to see the enlarged veins he had acquired from his lack of sleep.

"Yes Roy, that's what I'm telling you. That is how it is looking. Her family is filing a missing person's report. I need to know everything that you know, just in case there is anything else that is relevant."

"I've been thinking a lot about what we were talking about last time you came. Miss Hazel, I think my boss did something to Angela. They definitely had an argument the day before she didn't return to work, and now you're telling me she is missing? Something is not right. What if Angela knew about Mr. Waters' crimes and threatened to turn the information over to the FBI, and he killed her to cover it up? Do you think that is what actually happened?"

"I hate to say it, but that is certainly a possibility. I'm going to ask, for your own safety, that you keep this between us for now. Mr. Waters is a powerful man. If what we believe is true, he is also a very dangerous man. I'm going to keep digging and trying to find proof. Stay strong, Roy. I'm not giving up on you. Just keep hanging in there."

She felt terrible leaving him in that state, but she hoped to find the evidence that would set him free. That was her goal. She saw hope in his face as she left him that day, and he finally took a bite of his sandwich as she was leaving the conference room.

She sent a text to Tate. She needed to share what she had found out so far, and wanted to get some guidance as to what she should do next. Being a police officer, he should be able to guide her to what other avenues she could safely navigate to help Roy, as well as Angela. Not to mention, she really just wanted to see him again.

* * *

Before heading back home, she made her way to a friend of an acquaintance who was Wicca, to ask her more about the necklace she had seen on Angela in pictures and in spirit. Although she wasn't all that familiar with Wicca as a religion, her acquaintance told her the woman who she was going to see had a deep understanding of gemstone mysticism. The memory of Angela's that she had dreamed about made the necklace seem important, so she wanted to know all she could about the significance of the stone. She hoped this person could help her.

She pulled up to the small, simple cottage on

the outskirts of the city after only a short drive. Although it wasn't far from the city, it felt like it was from another world. From the outside, the house looked charming, with its wind chimes and birdhouses. It had a small garden and there were little wooden sculptures, carefully placed throughout the landscaped yard. Unlike many of the properties within the city that sported mostly roses or azaleas, this yard was filled with mostly wildflowers that were scattered throughout the yard as though their seeds took flight and sprouted where they landed. She could imagine it being a place where fairies could live happily, if only the mosquitos weren't big enough to eat them.

She pulled her keys out of the ignition and stepped out of her car. With hesitation, she climbed the stairs of the porch and knocked lightly on the purple front door. While waiting for her host to come to the door, she chewed nervously on her bottom lip. Just when she was about to turn around and leave, the door opened.

The woman who opened the door was nothing like she had imagined. She released the tension she had been holding in her body and snickered on the inside when she thought about how she expected a green, wart-nosed woman with a pointy hat and a hunched back to answer. Instead, the woman who answered the door was older, possibly in her mid to late seventies, but she was still beautiful. She had long, straight blond hair that went down her back, and clear blue eyes. She dressed in what could only be described as Bohemian garb. She had on two layers of long, loose skirts, one in brown and the other in ivory. She wore a navy-blue blouse covered with a long ivory lace vest. It looked like an effortless style, at least for her. The woman smiled from ear to ear when she saw her, which put Hazel instantly at ease.

"It's going to rain soon, dear. Let's go inside," the woman announced, as she shuffled back through the door, expecting Hazel to follow. As Hazel followed the woman inside, she was instantly enveloped in the scent of sweet basil.

"Thank you for seeing me today, Miss... I'm sorry I didn't catch your name."

The elderly woman didn't seem to hear her

and continued making her way into the kitchen, her skirts fluttering at her ankles as she walked.

"Tea, dear?"

The lady spoke in more of a song than a question, although she didn't wait for an answer, and instead started grabbing tea bags.

"Yes, ma'am, thank you."

"Well, sit right there in my tearoom, and I'll be right in with some tea."

Hazel did as she was told and sat down in the room towards the back of the house. The room that was referred to as the tearoom held a plethora of Wicca artifacts. There was so much to look at. Hazel's eyes darted around the room, trying to take it all in, while she listened to pots banging from the kitchen. There were pentagrams, moon shaped pieces, an object in the shape of a heart, and even a large branch that had bunches of dried herbs hanging from it. She walked up and gave each bundle a sniff, which sent an intoxicating mixture of fragrances into her nose.

"Teatime is here."

The lady sang as she walked into the room

carrying a silver tray with two teacups and a plate of cookies. She sat down on the chair next to Hazel.

"So, what brings you to me, dear?"

"My name is Hazel, and I was hoping you could tell me a little about a specific precious stone. I didn't catch your name though."

"Nice to meet you, Hazel. My name is Celeste. I'd be happy to help you with understanding your stone. What does the stone look like?"

Hazel explained what Angela's sapphire necklace looked like, while Ms. Celeste listened attentively. Saying nothing, she got out of her chair and walked over to a hutch across the room, and then came back with a velvet box. When she opened the box, it was filled with a variety of gemstones and crystals. She pulled out a sapphire with a star in the middle, similar to the one in Angela's necklace.

"This stone is called The Star Sapphire. The star you see in the middle represents the manifestation of divine knowledge and light into denser reality. It reminds us that the outer manifestations we treasure reflect the light of our own essence. The three lines that cross in the six-rayed star represent faith, hope and destiny. They are sometimes associated with three angels who offer protection to those who wear the Star Sapphire. The moving star brings ongoing safety to travelers and guides their way home."

Celeste explained the significance of the stone as though she recited the mysterious qualities of the Star Sapphire regularly.

Still confused, Hazel reached out her hand to hold the stone, so Celeste placed it carefully in her hand so she could examine it. Gemstones, Wicca and Mysticism were not in Hazel's wheelhouse, although, because of her gift, some would have thought otherwise. She didn't know the first thing about any of it, but she would learn if doing so would help Angela and Roy.

She carefully returned the stone to Celeste's waiting hands and debated if she wanted to verbalize her last question, when she finally decided to come out with it. Celeste had almost certainly dealt with stranger things than what she had to ask her.

"Can I ask you one more question?"

"Anything, my dear."

"If there was someone who wore a Star Sapphire all the time, if it was a family heirloom, for example, and it was stolen from them, and then their life was taken, what do you think would happen to their spirit?"

Hazel wondered if her ramble had even been understandable, but Celeste appeared to have understood.

"That's a very specific question, my dear. Did this happen to someone that you know?" Celeste asked quizzically.

"I'm afraid that it did. That is why I'm trying to find this out."

Celeste reached beside her chair and started reading through what appeared to be an ancient book, flipping through pages at what seemed to be entirely random. Hazel sat uncomplainingly, hoping that Celeste could give her some sort of answer to her complex question.

"It's hard to say, but if the owner of the Star Sapphire was given the stone, then they may be Wicca, and, without the stone, their spirit may be lost and confused. That would, of course, depend on how the stone was used by their family."

She acted as though she understood what Ms. Celeste was saying, but in reality, she had little a clue. She left, having slightly more of an understanding of why Angela had not crossed over, but it didn't get her any closer to solving Angela's murder. But she had bigger things to worry about that night, because she had to head home to meet up with Tate, and she was worried about the visit. She was going to share the paperwork she had found at Angela's mom's house with him, but she was also debating whether it was time for her to tell him about her abilities. Her stomach was in knots at the thought of it. It scared her that he would think she was crazy, and that he would leave and never come back. But she didn't know of any other way to get to the next level of her investigation into Angela's disappearance without telling Tate the truth. Scared of the possible aftermath, she didn't know how she was going to tell him, even though she knew she had to.

* * *

Tate met up with her at her apartment later that night. He was dressed in civilian clothes, which made it clear she had caught him on his day off. She always thought he looked handsome in his service uniform, but she, in fact, found him even cuter in his street clothes. Last time she had seen him, he'd asked her to call him so they could hang out, for a movie or something. Yet here she was contacting him, again, for 'official business.' She would not get out of the friend zone like that.

No matter the reason for the visit, he still came in and gave her a big bear hug. Unexpectedly, things seemed a bit more awkward between them, or maybe it was all in her head. He looked too good for her to spend their night only questioning him about police business. He had on a sexy navy-blue V-neck with a pair of dark wash jeans and brown leather boots. His face had been recently shaved, which allowed her to relish in the smell of his aftershave. She felt a flutter in her chest when he walked into her door, but she hoped her face hadn't revealed it to him. She realized he had put effort into his appearance before coming to see her, but she also realized she should have at least washed her hair, or maybe even brushed her teeth. This was why she was single, she thought to herself.

Candy swooped in behind him, without his knowledge, and pretended to smack him on the butt. Hazel had to fight to stifle back her laughter. She hurried to right her face before he looked up from taking off his shoes.

"You look tired, Hazel. Are you sleeping?" he asked, with a worried look on his face.

"He's so hot when he's concerned," Candy whispered into her ear, but Hazel did her best to ignore her.

"I'm trying. I just keep having these vivid nightmares that wake me up and leave me too startled to fall back asleep quickly. I could definitely afford to sleep more. But hey, thanks for the compliment."

Smirking, she shut the door behind him.

"I'm assuming you didn't invite me over for a social call, sadly, so what's going on?"

She explained everything she had found out

about Angela, and then showed him the paperwork she had found in Angela's old bedroom. She told him she suspected Raymond Waters was responsible for Angela's disappearance. The one thing she didn't tell him was that Angela's ghost had been guiding her on her quest, because she didn't want him to think she was crazy. She wasn't actually ready to let him in on her secret, but she really needed for him to be fully into her fold, so she was going to have to tell him.

"Tate."

"Yea?"

"Can you sit down with me? I need to talk to you about something important."

Her nerves intensified and she fought back her instinct to keep her secret.

"Of course," he told her as he wrapped his arm around her shoulders. His touch caused her to second guess her plan to tell him, but she decided she had no choice but to go through with it. She was at the point of sink or swim, all or nothing. If he was going to think she was crazy, and run out of the apartment like there was a fire, better he do it now than when she's even more head over heels for him.

Walking him over to the living room, her nerves buzzed like bees in her belly. Shoving two days of laundry onto one side of the sofa, she sat on the center cushion so he could sit next to her.

"So, there's something that I need to tell you, but I'm afraid you won't understand. I don't want you to think that I'm crazy. I just need for you to keep an open mind. Can you please do that for me?"

She searched his face for some sign of what he was thinking, but she couldn't read him, so she started tapping her foot nervously.

"Hazel, I care about you. I am always going to be here for you. Of course, I'm going to hear you out and keep an open mind. I can see that something is bothering you, so please tell me what is going on. Never worry that I'll think you are crazy. I know you are crazy, but I'm still here," he said, with a smile, as he pretended to punch her in the arm. "Just kidding. You know I'm here for you. I always will be."

She let out a deep breath and braced for what was to come, resigning to sharing her secret.

"I can see spirits and I can speak to spirits."

She paused, unsure of how he would react at the start. His face revealed the shock he was feeling, but he kept his composure, which she appreciated. He waited for her to continue.

"I can see spirits. I have since I was a child. It's a gift that was passed down on my mother's side of the family. They communicate with me and that is how I know about Angela. She has been coming to me and wants me to find out what happened to her. I'm sorry I never told you before. I just didn't want you to think that I was crazy."

She felt her cheeks turn red as she waited for his response. She looked down, unable to meet his line of sight.

"I've just never had much luck when coming clean with it to people."

She finally lifted her eyes, and he met her glance. He placed his hand on her still bouncing leg. She hadn't realized it was still bobbing, so she felt a bit embarrassed.

"Wow. I don't think you are crazy but, wow. That is hard to believe. I've just never met anyone who could do that before."

"I get that response a lot, but, usually worse, which is why I don't tend to tell people. I can prove it to you though."

"You can? How?"

"There is a spirit here now. She knows you."

"Really? Who? Where?"

Tate's head looked like it was on a swivel as he peered around the room with his eyes wide, but he turned up empty. She pointed straight ahead of them at the large blue chair across the room.

"She's sitting on that chair right there. Her name is Candy and she haunts my apartment. She was murdered here, but she says that you tried to save her life that night. She's a very flirty, royal pain in my ass. She also said you are a true gentleman, oh, and she would 'climb you like a tree' if she was still alive."

He let out a chuckle at being told about Candy's dirty comment, while simultaneously turning as white as a sheet of paper.

"Candy is here? I remember her. Oh, my god.

That was such a sad case. They called me to the scene. I tried to save her, but her injuries were too severe. Wow. This is heavy shit, Hazel. How do you handle this every day? No wonder you have nightmares."

Tate pulled her into a warm embrace. She sank into his arms, close enough that she could smell his aftershave. It was intoxicating. She let her eyes roll back in her head for just a moment. She could have spent the rest of the night in his arms, but she didn't think either of them was ready for that just yet, so she pulled away.

"It's difficult. Candy has become one of my only friends, besides you. She's a great friend, and she definitely helps me with the other spirit visitations. Angela has been haunting me in my apartment, in public, and even in my dreams, so I really need to figure out what happened to her, sooner rather than later. She isn't going to let me rest until I do. Do you think you can push some things along down at the station to get Mr. Waters looked at for her disappearance?"

"I can try. Mr. Waters has a lot of power in this city. If what you are telling me is true, he's also dangerous. You need to stop digging into him. Let me see what I can find out by doing my own investigation. I don't want you to get hurt, or worse, end up missing like Angela. Make copies of this paperwork and send it to the station, anonymously. I don't want you at risk if anyone finds out you are responsible for possibly taking down one of the most influential men in this city. I'll get back to you soon, but please be careful until then. I need for you to stay safe, so that I can eventually get that date."

He winked at her.

"Climb me like a tree, huh? Did she really say that?"

He let out a chuckle, disarming her slightly.

"Yup! Welcome to my life. She's always like that."

Hazel rolled her eyes as he wrapped his arm around her shoulders. They both laughed.

"Well, it's really sad what happened to her, but it sounds like she's making the best of it."

"And annoying me along the way."

He hugged her and kissed her forehead. She wished she had Candy's courage, so she could have tilted her face upwards and planted one right on his lips, but she couldn't, at least not yet. When he walked out of her apartment, she felt her heart flood with emotion. For the first time, she actually thought she could have a chance with him, just maybe. She hoped he felt the same way.

"Swoon!" Candy exclaimed, as she fluttered over like a fiery-haired cherub. "If you aren't going to make a move on him, you don't deserve to have him. He likes you! Please tell me you're going to go out with him eventually!"

"I don't know, Candy. I've known Tate for so long, and honestly, I don't think he'd be interested in me as soon as he got close enough to see how much of an undomesticated mess I really am. Obviously I like him. I have for a long time. But I'd rather have him as a friend than not have him at all."

"To be honest, Hazel, I don't think Tate would ever stop being your friend, even if a love life didn't work out for you two. The two of you go way back. I think it's safe to say that he'd be in it for the long haul. And don't be so hard on yourself. He knows that you're an absolute train wreck, but he still keeps coming at your beck and call. I don't think you can scare him away. Give him a chance. You've been alone for a long time. You need someone in your life, other than me."

"Thanks Candy. You know, sometimes you're an enlightening friend. Other times, you really are a pain in my ass. What I can't figure out is if you really think Tate and I could be something special, or if you just want me to have sex with him so you can see him naked. Plus, you know you are my one true love."

Candy blew her a kiss with her perfectly penciled red lips. Hazel pretended to catch it and put it into her pocket.

"I love you too, but, if I were alive, I'd absolutely want a piece of that! Unfortunately, I can't have him, but you can. And come on, I'm being serious about you and him getting together. I think he'd be good for you. He seems to have his shit together. Plus, he totally might just already love you. I bet he's totally hot naked though."

Hazel forced a scowl.

"Hey! Don't even try to picture that! And I doubt he loves me."

"Okay, whatever you say, but you never know. Anyway, maybe he'd be an excellent role model? He can help you get things tidy. Stop selling yourself short. Anyway, doll, what's your plan after speaking to him? Are you still going to pursue digging into this murder, even if you may get yourself whacked too?"

"I don't think Angela is going to let me back off of this investigation, even if I wanted to. She will continue to haunt my dreams and pop up in front of me until I help her. I know Tate is right, and Waters is dangerous, but I have an obligation to help her. This is what I was born to do. So, I cannot back off, but I can be careful."

"Oh, come on. When have you ever been careful? I don't like it, Hazel. I really think you should listen to Tate. You really are in over your head."

"I know my track record isn't that great, so I'll rephrase and say I'll try to be careful, but I have to keep going."

* * *

Sleep was like a goal that Hazel couldn't reach that night. Candy was right, she was in over her head. She was starting to feel like she was drowning, and it wasn't a good feeling, but she didn't know what else to do. Angela hadn't appeared in her bedroom again, but she knew it was only a matter of time if she didn't make headway in Angela's disappearance case. Spirits could be pretty persistent. They didn't have to follow the same rules that living people followed, including simple ones, like not being able to walk through locked doors. They pretty much just did whatever they wanted to do. She did not want Angela to make a habit of showing up at the foot of her bed, so she was going to do her best to at least appear as though she was making progress on the case.

Lying in bed that night, she drifted in and out of sleep, never falling in too deep for more than a few hours. Her racing thoughts kept her awake, and her fear of more memory-induced nightmares kept her awake, so she was fighting a losing battle with her mind, and with Angela's.

6

Challenges
and the
Visit

Bits and pieces of visions flashed through my mind, almost too fast for me to make out what they were. When the world stopped spinning, I looked around and could finally see clearly, although I didn't know how I had gotten there. Sitting on the forest floor, my body covered in mud, I gazed around and saw only swampland. I called out for help, but my voice only

echoed back to me. A flock of birds scattered in the distance as the water of the swamp splashed, almost like something had fallen into it. Climbing to my feet, I stumbled over to the water's edge and peered into the water, hoping I wouldn't find an alligator staring back at me. The reflection in the rippling water horrified me because the face staring back at me wasn't my face at all.

* * *

Hazel woke up to Candy petting her hair and whispering lovingly to her.

"You're okay, Hazel. Wake up, love. It's okay."

Hazel, confused, tried to sit up, only to find it was more difficult than she had expected.

"Hey, Candy. What's going on?"

"You were just having another nightmare, love. I was trying to wake you up."

Hazel rubbed her eyes sleepily and laid back down, pulling her covers up to her chin.

"Oh. Thanks. I'm exhausted."

Hazel stifled a yawn.

"I bet. You didn't sleep much last night."

"I feel it. Thankfully I don't have to be in court today."

"No? Well, that's good. Maybe you can get some rest then."

"I think I'm going to see if Tate wants to hang out... he keeps asking."

"Ooh. That's a great idea. Maybe you should shower first."

Candy smiled, pointing at Hazel's greasy hair.

Tossing her covers off, Hazel forced herself out of bed and into the bathroom, grabbing her phone along the way. Knowing Tate was scheduled for the night shift, she texted him to ask him if he was available to come by for a few hours so they could hang out, and not for business reasons. Although she was expecting rejection, he accepted her offer, so her insides abruptly felt like a she was on a roller coaster. She hoped she could calm her nerves before he showed up.

While grabbing the towel to wash her face, she noticed a shadow on the other side of the shower curtain.

"Candy?"

She spoke in a low voice, expecting Candy to speak from just on the other side of the curtain. Instead, Candy floated into the room, causing the shadow to disperse.

"You called?"

"Oh, I thought I heard you."

"No, but don't forget to wash that hair."

Hazel made a mimicking face behind the curtain.

"I will. Thanks."

"Okay, doll. See you when you're out," Candy replied, as she left.

The shadow was gone, but Hazel felt uneasy. She washed her hair quickly and then turned off the water to get out of the shower. When she opened the shower curtain to climb out, she saw him. A man, the same man she had seen in her bathroom mirror only days before, was standing in front of her, bleeding on her bathroom rug. He appeared to be in shock. She could feel the emotions flowing off of him like an electrical current. He shivered violently as he dripped. She wrapped the towel around herself and carefully stepped out of the shower, inching slightly closer to him.

"I can help you. What is your name?"

He continued to stare at her, trembling. His eyes watched her movements, but he didn't speak, as his stab wounds bled profusely on her bathroom floor, making puddles at her feet. Suddenly, he started breathing rapidly, shaking more violently. Startled by his frantic movements, she ran right through him and out of the bathroom, pausing only momentarily as she felt the icy air touch her skin. Once she got to her bedroom, she sat down on the bed, watching the bathroom door, relieved he did not follow her. Her heart continued to pound as she tried to calm herself down. Candy, noticing her distress, came to sit next to her.

"Are you okay? Hazel, what's wrong?"

"A man. There was a man in the bathroom."

Before she was finished speaking, Candy had already floated to the bathroom door to look for the intruder, but she returned just as fast with a puzzled look on her face.

"There's no one there, love."

Hazel calmed her breathing.

"It was a spirit. He's probably long gone by now."

Candy furrowed her brow, glancing back towards the open bathroom door.

"I just don't like how much they are coming into our apartment now. I hope this doesn't become a regular thing. Have you seen this guy before?"

"Yes."

"Where did you see him? And when?"

Candy's tone had hardened, sending Hazel's heart into her stomach. She had never told Candy about the man in the mirror and she never intended to, because she didn't want to worry her. She bit her lip tensely as she planned her next words carefully.

"In the bathroom, a few weeks ago, but he disappeared quickly."

Her eyes cast down to the floor. She knew she shouldn't have kept it from Candy.

"Why didn't you tell me, Hazel?"

Hazel shrugged.

"I don't know. I was just busy that morning

and never got around to it. It wasn't intentional. It was the same morning Angela's spirit showed up at the end of my bed, so I was already feeling distressed."

Candy's look softened, although her voice still held a sternness to it.

"Well, please tell me about these things from now on. We share this apartment together. I'd like to know when we have unexpected guests. I know it had been a difficult day for you, but I could have possibly helped you with him."

"I will. I'm sorry. He really did disappear quickly though, so he would have been gone by the time I called you in."

Before she could dwell anymore about the bleeding man in her bathroom, a knock on the door brought a much-needed distraction. Still in a towel, she threw on a robe and ran to the door, with a towel still wrapped around her hair.

Opening the door, she kept the chain lock still in place, and Tate's smiling face was staring right back at her.

"Oh, hello," she said sheepishly, tugging at her robe.

"Are you going to just leave me out here," he asked, holding up a brown paper bag. "I brought food."

Closing the door so she could unlatch the chain, she opened the door all the way to allow him to enter. Slightly embarrassed, she stood behind the door as he walked in.

"I just got out of the shower, so I'm going to throw some clothes on."

She scurried down the hall and into her bedroom.

Candy, floating in behind her, tried desperately to get her to put on lingerie, but Hazel scoffed at the idea. Grabbing a pair of yoga pants, which was Candy's second choice, and an oversized tee-shirt, she made her way back into the living room where she was surprised to see that Tate had laid out lunch for them on her small kitchen table. He looked up at her and smiled.

"I didn't know what you liked, so I grabbed a few things. I figured you hadn't eaten yet."

"You figured correct. Thank you! And I'll eat just about anything."

She sat down in the chair he had pulled out for her.

"You didn't have to do all of this, Tate."

"I know, but I wanted to," he responded, as he pulled out his own chair.

He had brought them soups and sandwiches from a shop right around the corner from her house. She was a pickier eater than she had led on, but the food from that shop was actually fantastic, so he had chosen well.

"So, what are you up to today?" he asked, while taking a bite out of his sandwich.

Hazel, with a mouth full of bread, had to finish chewing before she answered.

"I don't have to be in court today, so I planned to look through all of that paperwork that I snatched from Angela's mom's house."

"Have you given any thought to what I said about Raymond Waters? I just don't want you getting hurt."

"I know, and I don't either. But I've been helping spirits for my entire life, and I know Angela will not let me just forget about her and move on with my life."

He reached over to hold her hand.

"Look, I can't pretend to understand how this works for you, your gift, as you call it. The thing about Angela is really sad, and I hope they find her. But my concern is for you. You are my friend. You are who I care about."

She suddenly found it difficult to meet his eye and, instead, stared at her hand in his.

"I'm sorry that I'm making you worried. Candy is worried too. It's the last thing I want. I don't want to cause either of you more stress. I can't give up on Angela, but I'm going to be careful. I promise."

"I trust you," he said, while gently squeezing her hand.

She smiled on the outside, but on the inside, she was traveling down a spiral of self-doubt.

They finished their lunch without saying much else. She didn't know what else to say. She didn't like that she was causing him to worry about her. She thought, for a moment, that maybe this was why her parents had issues. Maybe her mother had allowed spirits to get her into more precarious situations than her father could handle, but she couldn't be sure. It made her second guess ever getting into a relationship at all, if all she would ever do was make her partner worry. She hated to think about her future in that way, but she'd never been one to look on the bright side, anyway.

After lunch, Hazel settled in to go through her paperwork, and Tate headed out to get a nap before his night shift. He hugged her goodbye, as he always did, but she couldn't help but feel more distant, not because she wanted to be, but because she didn't want to hurt him, or to ruin their friendship by complicating it. She hated feeling like things were so awkward between them when he left, but she really needed to focus on her case, so her self-doubts would have to wait until later.

Sitting down at the kitchen table with stacks of documents strewn around in front of her made her feel the need for anxiety medication or a drink, neither of which she had. She was certainly not qualified to understand most of the jargon on the financial paperwork, aside from what she had learned during her schooling to become an attorney. She felt clueless. She would have to give her undivided attention to the paperwork to make sense of it. Putting on a pot of coffee, she had her work cut out for her, and she was dreading every second of it.

Before she even went through the first page, the phone rang, startling her.

"Hello, Miss Hazel? This is Sylvia."

"Oh, hi, Sylvia. Any news on the missing person's case?"

"Well, at first, the chief of police did not want to take it seriously, because he said that Angela was an adult, and she could disappear if she chose to. I refused to let it go that easy. I told him that Angela wouldn't just run off knowing how ill her mother was, and he finally agreed to file the report and pursue the case. He said he would file the paperwork today and it would be shared on the news for tips."

"Okay, good. At least that is a little progress. I also spoke to a friend of mine who is on the police force. He is going to look into some things as well. Thank you for the calling me and keeping me in the loop. How is Mrs. Harriet doing?"

"Mrs. Harriet is doing about the same. She seems content as long as she is sitting by the window. I haven't told her about Angela's disappearance, because I don't think she would understand me, but she seems agitated lately. It has been getting harder to put her to sleep at night, but her doctor came by and prescribed her a sedative. There have been no changes otherwise."

"I'm so sorry to hear that she is feeling so unsettled at night. I hope that things with Angela become resolved soon so Mrs. Harriet can hopefully feel more at peace."

"We can only pray."

"Yes, ma'am."

"Well, I won't keep you any longer. Please call with any other updates and I will do the same."

"Yes, ma'am. Will do. Talk to you soon. Bye."

She hung up the phone, feeling less pressure on her shoulders. With any luck, the police would find Angela's body, and she could move on with her life. She couldn't see where

Angela's murder could be pinned on Roy, so she didn't feel that she had a reason to worry about that possibility. If anything, solving Angela's murder would exonerate Roy. Well, that was the hope.

By the time the five o'clock news came on, Angela's face was plastered on the television with a phone number to call for anyone who had any information that could help find her. The one thing that worried Hazel was that the news story would make Raymond Waters become paranoid and possibly more dangerous. She still intended to meet with him in the upcoming days, but didn't want him to lash out at her. She wasn't yet sure how she could meet with him and stay off his radar at the same time.

The darkness seemed to fall more quickly that night. Maybe it was because of the pouring rain, or maybe it was because she knew the body of an innocent woman was out there, somewhere, and whether it was found directly affected her life, not to mention the fate of the woman's spirit. With an active search, it had become much more likely that Angela's body would be found, which was a relief, but it also made her a target if Raymond Waters discovered she was behind starting the search. She didn't see any way she could separate herself from those two scenarios, although she would have preferred to not be a part of any of them. She would have given anything for a normal, boring life.

Later that night, as she relaxed on her sofa, watching reruns of black and white sitcoms, just as she was dozing off, three heavy bangs sounded at her front door. She sat up quickly, and sleepily looked around the living room for Candy, knowing that Candy would have heard the noise as well. Before she even had a chance to call out for her, Candy came into the room from somewhere in the back of the apartment.

"Did you hear the beating on the door? Can you peak and see who it is?" Hazel asked.

Candy nodded her head in acknowledgment before sliding right through the wall next to the front door. She returned quickly with a troubled look on her face.

"Hazel, don't answer the door or make any noise. That's John. Something isn't right."

Candy eyes were wide. She was afraid.

"Angela's ex-husband, John?"

Hazel felt completely puzzled, wondering why John would be at her front door.

"Yes! He looks drunk. Don't open the door. It's not worth it. You can call him tomorrow."

"Candy, I need to speak to him. I'll just open it, but I'll leave the chain lock closed. Back me up. I need to know what he wants. It could be important."

"Hazel, how does he even know where you live? Don't chance it."

Candy begged but Hazel did not mirror her fears. Ignoring the last question, she walked to the door, making sure the chain lock was still on as she cracked the door open. John looked disheveled.

"What's going on, John? Why are you here? It's late."

"You came to my house looking for Angela and now I'm the prime suspect in her disappearance. What did you tell the cops? I didn't touch her!"

"John, I never spoke to the police about you,

or Angela. If someone has reported her missing, her ex-husband would be the first person who they looked into. If you are innocent, then you should just maintain your innocence and work to get your name cleared. I met with her mother's home health nurse and told her how cooperative you've been. I, in no way, made them think that you were a suspect. They filed the missing person's report because she is missing, and it was the right thing to do. I would have thought you would have understood that. Cooperate with the investigation. If you did nothing wrong, then you shouldn't worry."

"I swear to you, Hazel, you'd better not be behind this! How dare you knock on my door and then turn my life upside down. I loved Angela! You'd better hope I don't get charged with something that I didn't do!"

And with that last threat, John stormed off, got into his truck, and sped away. Hazel closed and locked the door, feeling more panicked than she had led on in front of John.

"Wow, Hazel. That was crazy. Do you think he did something to Angela?"

"I really don't. Sylvia told me they ended on bad terms, but Angela has given me no clues to make me believe he was behind this. It does sound like they had a toxic marriage, though, and he has an alcohol problem. It's hard to rule anyone out completely, but after all the stuff Roy told me about Angela's issues with their boss, I really don't see how John could have been involved. Come and look at this."

Candy followed her to the table that was now covered with a mountain of documents.

"Look at these bank statements that Angela kept. She highlighted through all of them, only certain accounts. Something is here. I just know it. Why would Angela keep this stuff hidden at her mom's house? Even after her death, she was still trying to get to this stuff. I think I need to meet Angela's old boss, Raymond Waters, and I need to find the energy to go through more of this paperwork before I have to turn it over to the police."

"But what if he's dangerous, Hazel? If he hurt Angela, you could be next. The minute you get into his sights, you could make yourself a target. I don't want you to end up like me."

"I won't. I'm not going to meet up with him alone. I'll make sure that there are other people around and I'll make sure it's under the guise of me as Roy's attorney. I'm not intending to go interrogate him or anything."

"I think you should listen to Tate and wait. There's no reason to rush, Hazel. Angela is already dead. Let the police do their job and just bide your time for now."

"There's no harm in just meeting with him as an attorney for his former employee. That's all I'm going to do. He will never know that I suspect him of anything."

Just as Hazel had stated it, even she hadn't believed it. Part of her knew that going to see Waters would be dangerous, and she would be forever putting herself onto his radar, but she didn't believe she had a choice. It wasn't like Angela had given her an option about whether she could ignore this murder investigation. The minute Angela showed up at the foot of her bed in the middle of the night, she made it clear that

Hazel only had one choice in the matter, and that was to help her. She only wished that Angela was a bit more helpful in her own case. Angela's cryptic messaging and traumatizing memories weren't helping anyone.

Hazel's phone vibrated on the kitchen counter, nearly making her jump out of her skin. Her nerves were really on edge, but she tried to simmer them down for Tate's sake.

"Hey, Tate. What's up?"

"Hey, Hazel. Sorry for calling so late. I hope I didn't wake you."

"No. I was still awake and talking to Candy."

"Oh. That's going to take some getting used to. I guess... tell her hi for me?"

The tone of his voice made her smile.

"That's understandable and I can absolutely do that. I'm sure she'll have some perverted response for you. So, what's going on?"

He chuckled.

"Well, I tried to check into Angela's case to see if they are looking into Raymond, but the case is being kept close to the vest. I'm not able to find out much at all, unfortunately. I will keep my eyes and ears open, though. Something will slip out eventually, it always does. I saw that the missing person's case was filed though, so that should help a lot."

"Okay. I understand. Thank you for trying and yea, I spoke to her mother's caregiver recently, and she filled me in on her conversation with the police. It sounds like they are taking the case seriously, although they tried to dismiss her at first, something about Angela being old enough to disappear if she wanted to."

"Yea, unfortunately, it's hard to know sometimes if people are really missing, or if they left their lives in order to start a new one. Unless she were a juvenile, they would usually want a bit more proof that something happened to her, and that she didn't leave of her own accord. Hey, don't forget to make copies of that paperwork and send it in. That may be what breaks this case wide open."

"I definitely will. I want to go through it a bit more, but I will get it out soon. I'm hoping there is something important contained in there I can use, but I do plan to send it off within the next few days. I have to believe Angela kept it, and led me to it, for a good reason."

"I agree. Well, I'll let you get to bed, but talk soon?"

"Yea, sure. Call me whenever. Good night, Tate."

"Good night, Hazel."

A warm sensation passed throughout her as she hung up the phone. Something about Tate did that to her. She only wished she could tell him, but she was much too afraid. It was a flaw she needed to work on. Although she was fearful that pursuing a romantic relationship with him would hurt their friendship, she couldn't deny that the feelings were there, and they were strong. It made her wonder what was worse, chancing losing him as a friend, or suffering without ever being with him, and being forced to watch him eventually end up with someone else. She couldn't bear the thought of that; it made her feel sick to her stomach to think of him with someone else.

"Ooh, was that your lover boy?" Candy purred, with her hands perched under her chin, which made her look like a dreamy-eyed schoolgirl.

"Good night, Candy."

Hazel headed towards her bedroom, trying to hide the flush of her cheeks. Candy would have undoubtedly teased her nonstop if she would have seen how much she was blushing.

She had a hard time clearing her head that night. So many things had happened in the previous few weeks since starting Roy's case. The ride seemed never-ending, and it was burning her out. After clearing most of her schedule from appointments and obligations, except those to do with Roy, she still felt she had too many things to manage. Even her visit with Celeste circled in her mind as she thought about their last conversation. Celeste told her that Angela's spirit may be lost or confused without her Star Sapphire, if it had been taken from her when she died. Hazel worried that, even if Angela's body was found, what if her necklace wasn't with her body? How would she find this woman's necklace? Where was she even supposed to look? Of course, it would have been great if the necklace would still be on Angela's neck. However, the last few times she'd seen Angela, the spectral necklace flickered when Angela touched it, which seemed unusual. Not to mention the spirit seemed to always be touching her necklace. It was almost like Angela was trying to tell her something was wrong, and the necklace was part of the key to helping her, but she did not know how to interpret Angela's cryptic signs. She also thought about the dream she had about Angela receiving the necklace from her dying grandmother, a dream that told her how important the necklace was to Angela, to her entire family.

All of those thoughts swirled in her mind, yet created mostly uncertainty. Angela's necklace may have still been on her body, but there was a chance that it wasn't, and if it wasn't, there was a chance her spirit would still not cross over, whether or not her body was found. If the fate of Angela's spirit, and the fate of Roy's future, wasn't enough to keep her mind from settling, she couldn't stop thinking about Tate either.

The more time she spent with him, the more she wanted to be with him, as more than a friend, but she didn't know if he wanted the same thing. The last thing she wanted to do was weigh anyone down; she already felt like she was holding Candy back from crossing over, and that was as much of a burden as she could handle being to someone she loved. She only wished that Tate would take the reins, and make the decision for her. Then, maybe, she could adjust to their new reality, whatever that may end up being.

Listening to the storm hit her bedroom window, she laid in bed while staring at the ceiling, trying to suppress her persistent thoughts. Angry at herself for never learning to meditate, she downloaded a relaxation app on her phone, and set it to play as it laid on the bed next to her. Finally, somewhere in the whirlwind that was her mind, her consciousness got lost, and she eventually succumbed to sleep, and all that waited for her on the other side.

7

Candy's Trick and the Evidence

Standing in the center of the room, she frantically watched as the vortex pulled everything not bolted down out through the window. Not recognizing where she was, she spun around dramatically, almost appearing as though she was being taken into the

vortex herself. She could almost see glimpses of familiar places on the other side of the window frame, but the swirling wind obstructed her view. Her heart raced as she tried to get her bearings, but she couldn't figure out where she was, or how she had gotten there. In a deafening boom, the room itself got sucked into the vortex, with her still inside. Screaming, she grabbed onto the built-in bookshelves, and held on for her life, as the whirlwind whipped her hair violently around her face. She closed her eyes and waited for the inevitable moment when she crashed back down.

* * *

Waking up in the morning, Hazel was so nauseated that she had to make herself vomit just to feel better. Just in case she was coming down with a stomach virus, she cleared her schedule, although she had a feeling she was only suffering the aftereffects of the intense nightmare that had plagued her in the night. It couldn't have been a memory. It felt more like she was experiencing the inside of someone's mind, maybe hers or maybe Angela's. She couldn't be sure, but she hoped it wasn't hers. The thought made her shiver. It was an unsettling thought to follow an unsettling experience.

Leading up to her call with Raymond Waters to schedule a meeting, she admittedly felt nervous. She didn't want to call right after returning from Mobile, because with the missing person's case hitting the news, she felt it best to let the dust settle. If he was Angela's killer, the news broadcasts would have undoubtedly agitated him, so she didn't want to fire him up more, at least not for a few days. She was so intimidated by him, although she had never even met him. She was worried she may end up retching on his shoes the minute he stepped in front of her, but she hoped that wouldn't be the case. She thought about asking Candy to go to his house with her, but Candy did not approve of her getting involved in Angela's murder investigation. Plus, she really felt like she needed to go alone. She was an adult and being an attorney was her job. He was setting up for a party, for goodness' sake. They wouldn't be alone, so there was no reason for her to bring the brigade along, or at least that is what she kept trying to tell herself. She would be okay.

Before meeting with Waters, she really wanted to go through some of the documentation Angela had hidden inside the wooden trunk at her mother's house. Hazel hoped it contained information that could help to exonerate her client, Roy Miller, or prove the guilt of Raymond Waters. But it was a huge undertaking. The paperwork collection was extensive. And Hazel, not being an accountant, did not feel qualified to analyze all of it, but she felt comfortable with her understanding of most of it. To make sense of it all, she had separated the various stacks of paperwork, from Waters' Financial Firm, into piles based on their categories. One of the first things she went through was the stack of bank statements, since she was familiar with that type of document. Angela had already done the work of going through the bank statements and highlighting most of the inconsistencies, so all Hazel needed to do was make sense of the items Angela had already drawn attention to. She felt thankful for Angela's diligent effort, and for having the day off to go through it, even though it started off so awful.

Enjoying the quiet of the morning, with Candy being somewhere out on the town, and not bouncing around the apartment, Hazel put on a pot of coffee and plopped herself onto the sofa in her comfiest pajamas, surrounded by bank statements. Not the most relaxing of settings, but it beat the courthouse any day. Hopefully, before the end of the day, she could find something to help Roy. Going through the highlighted transactions first, she decided it would be wise to look into the accounts where the highlighted deposits were being funneled.

Thumbing through and finding the first of the highlighted accounts that received a large deposit from the Waters company, she went online to see if the company was legit, but found that it was. Even so, she knew there had to have been a reason Angela highlighted the name. She wrote the name of Aberdeen's Trucking Company down and moved on to the next highlighted entry.

"Well, you're up early, sunshine. What are you up to?"

Candy strolled in from outside in the corridor. Hazel looked up at her and then pointed dramatically down to the papers that were strewn across the coffee table. It never failed that distractions were going to stop her from accomplishing what she needed to do, and it was frustrating.

"I'm trying to go through this stuff, but I only just got started, and it's already boring the hell out of me. What have you been doing all day?"

Collapsing onto the large chair across from Hazel, Candy cracked an ear-to-ear smile.

"I was just doing a little... um... window shopping," she hinted.

"Window shopping for what?"

Hazel narrowed her eyes at Candy, feeling curious. She could tell Candy was up to something.

Candy pursed her lips in a mischievous pucker and shot her eyes up towards the ceiling, darting them around as though she were trying to make her avoidance of eye contact obvious. Hazel could practically hear the 'la ti das' playing in her head.

"Candy... what did you do today?"

Hazel straightened her posture, eyes fixed on her impish friend.

Finally, after a few long moments, Candy looked back down at Hazel, who had become a ball of nerves, and smiled.

"Girl, you have got to calm down those nerves. How are you going to make it through a meeting with Raymond Waters if you can't even handle me telling you I went window shopping?" Candy quipped with a laugh.

"I know. I'm all wound up today. I'm sorry. I just have a lot to do."

Hazel brushed the hair out of her face and shook her head, looking back down at the paperwork in her lap.

"It's okay, doll."

"Wait a minute, you still didn't tell me what you did today."

"Oh, I mostly just followed Tate around after you went to bed last night," Candy teased with a grin.

Hazel, losing all ability to respond, simply stared at Candy, perplexed.

She finally attempted to get her jaw off of the floor, look as fierce as she could, and pull herself together.

"And why did you do that?" she demanded in the most serious tone she could muster.

Candy looked nonchalant, shifting ever so slightly in her chair. Hazel hardened her look.

"Just to see what he does all day," Candy clarified with a wave of her hand, "I wanted to make sure he was good enough for you."

"So, you weren't just trying to see him naked?"

Hazel arched an eyebrow, her stare deepening.

The question did not surprise Candy, and she smirked knowingly.

"Hey, if the opportunity arose... but no, that isn't why. I get bored when you're asleep, so I found something to do."

Hazel relaxed back into her seat, pulling her legs up under herself.

"Well, what did you see then, Miss Sherlock Holmes?"

Candy pretended to lower her nonexistent eyeglasses to the tip of her nose.

"It was elementary, my Dear Watson. He was an exquisite specimen to behold."

Hazel flared her nostrils and Candy took the hint.

"Okay. Okay. You don't have to breathe fire. I rode around with him in his cruiser for a while. I only played with his scanner a little... just to see if I could," she said playfully.

Hazel's eyebrows popped back up again, as though they were on a loaded spring.

"What do you mean? Did you scare him? You'd better not be trying to scare him."

Hazel looked horrified, but Candy giggled.

"No! Nothing like that! I just tried to speak through his scanner. I'd never tried it before. I thought it would be a helpful skill, if it would ever work."

Candy shrugged her shoulders. Her red locks bounced as though they were floating on air.

"And did it work?"

"Not at first... it's difficult to transform my

energy and get it into the proper channel... it was mostly only a whisper mixed with static, at first."

Hazel leaned in closer with her eyes wide.

"But you got it to work?"

"Yea, kind of. I mean, Tate heard something. I know he did. I'm not sure if he could make out exactly what I was saying, but it caught his attention. He even pulled the car over so he could turn the volume louder and turn the dial to improve the quality of the feed. I think with a little practice..."

"You could get messages to him?"

"Yea. I think so."

"Wow. Candy, that is so cool. It's pretty weird that you followed him... I'm still not sure how I feel about that," she gave Candy a sideways glance, "but it would be really cool if you could learn to communicate with the living like that. You never know when you may need to use that skill. But don't go scaring the shit out of him, okay?"

"I promise."

Candy pretended to draw a halo above her head. Hazel looked at her and smirked.

"Oh, Hazel."

"Yea?"

"I saw him naked. Just so you know."

Candy winked. Hazel's jaw dropped while her brain tried to process which emotion she needed to pull from. She didn't know if she should yell, laugh, or cry, so she didn't do any of them. Instead, her brain did its own version of a factory reset, as she sat there with a blank stare, feeling like a moron. Finally, once the reset was complete, and she put it into perspective, she realized she couldn't be mad at Candy, but that didn't mean she would let her off of the hook too easy. Candy couldn't be with men anymore, so she knew she couldn't expect her to not look at them either. However, she would prefer it if Candy kept her eyes on any other guy, just not Tate.

"You did what?"

Hazel pretended to be mad, although she wasn't, not really anyway.

"Relax, doll. It's not like I can have him or anything. He's all yours. Anyway, how was I supposed to know that he was going to strip down naked after work, right there in the locker room?"

She peered at Hazel with doe eyes, trying to look innocent, but Hazel wasn't buying it.

"What, on the planet, were you even doing in the locker room?"

Hazel felt her face turn red but Candy looked at her as though the answer was blatantly obvious.

"I was checking out the guys, duh!"

"Do you ever stop?"

"Only when I'm dead... oops... nope... never going to happen. I love you, though," Candy kidded, blowing Hazel a kiss, causing her to shake her head. She would usually catch the kisses and put them in her pocket for later, but not this time. This time, she was supposed to be mad.

"I can't believe that you saw him naked. I haven't even..."

"No, Hazel, I'm not going to tell you about it. No cheating. You'll have to just make a move if you want to know," Candy taunted with a shrug. "He's yours for the taking, if you'd ever get off of your butt and try, before someone else takes him."

Hazel, offended, threw a pillow at her, only to have her dissipate before it landed, causing the pillow to bounce off of the wall and onto the floor. Candy re-materialized on the sofa, sitting right next to her instead. Hazel flipped her off, for good measure, and then dramatically looked back down at the paperwork in front of her.

"Whatever. You're distracting me, anyway. I have to go through this paperwork. Do you want to help?"

"If you find something that is suited to my special talents, I am at your service," Candy replied with a salute.

"So, if I find a guy in my research, who needs a date? Got it."

Hazel rolled her eyes while repositioning herself on the sofa. Digging back into the paperwork now at her feet, she needed to get refocused, although her brain had moved to Tate land. She resumed her search through the highlighted deposits on the bank statements and found the second entry to be a company by the

name of R.L.F, Inc. She ran an internet search
for the company and could find no record of its
existence. Befuddled, she put an asterisk next
to it and moved on through the following pages,
looking to see if the same company had received
more deposits. Throughout the subsequent
stacks of statements, she found that R.L.F, Inc.
was listed dozens of times with deposits of
varying quantities. Scratching her head, she
gave the bank statements a rest and moved on
to the other paperwork piles. She hoped to find
something that could tell her more about who
or what R.L.F, Inc. was as a company, or at least
who they were to Waters' Financial Firm.

Looking through her other paperwork
options, Hazel thumbed through printouts of
emails and found one that mentioned the
Raymond Laura Fund. The email had been sent
from a man named Craig Donner, who appeared
to be from a bank that Hazel had never heard of.
The email said little, other than confirming that
the Raymond Laura Fund had been established.
Although that was all it said, something clicked
inside of her, telling her that this was the link

she needed to find, the link between Raymond Waters and the embezzlement of his own company. Maybe it was intuition, or maybe Angela was pointing her to that conclusion, but she felt it. She didn't know what he was doing with the money, but from the look of what she had in front of her, Raymond may have been funneling money into his own fund and passing it off as legitimate business deposits, although she couldn't be sure. She wasn't qualified to say that the fund wasn't a legitimate charity. She would need to send the paperwork to the FBI, or someone else who was qualified to analyze the data. She did, however, feel better now that she had looked over the paperwork herself. It gave her a little more confidence to know inside information that the district attorney did not know, and every bit of confidence counted.

* * *

Pictures flash through her unconscious mind as though she was looking through a View Finder. Pictures of women, four of them, all dressed differently, but the only one she recognizes is Angela. The photos were all taken near the swamp. She could tell by the way the trees grew from the murky water. In some of the pictures, a woman is lying down in the mud, but in others, she is sitting by a tree. The Star Sapphire sparkles in the sunlight as she holds it in her hand. White flags flap in the wind as rain pelts the waterlogged ground beneath them. The pictures begin to move faster, increasing speed until they are moving too fast for her to make out anything more than a blur.

* * *

Hazel woke up to the tap of raindrops on her window, but the rain had passed by the time she had finished her coffee. She had gotten an appointment to meet with Raymond Waters fairly easily. He was throwing a dinner party a few days after her call and agreed to let her stop by for a few questions before the party started. So, leading up to their appointment, she made sure she had a proper clean suit and freshly washed hair. She needed to at least look the part of a successful attorney.

Before her meeting with him, she and Candy had made a plan to check out one of the main Voodoo shops downtown, to see if there was a way to keep the unwanted spirits out of their apartment. The uptick of unwanted guests had made both of them uncomfortable, so they were both trying to think of ways in which to taper down the flow. Hazel wasn't convinced that anything would work, but she humored Candy's idea anyway, and agreed to go to the shop.

She drove up to the shop and eyed it cautiously. Candy had brought up a good point, ironically, and told her spirits needed boundaries, but Hazel wasn't really comfortable messing with things she didn't understand.

She argued with herself about going inside, about whether she was committing to something she couldn't fulfill. She laughed at the idea that it was like a contract, like there were terms and conditions at the end of the page, but then she hoped it wasn't. She reasoned with herself that going into the shop and asking a few questions didn't mean she had to agree to use their methods. She was just there to check it out. There was no harm in that.

"Come on... where's your sense of adventure?" Candy asked, as she was outside of the car with her head poking in through the passenger side window, unfazed by the solid pane of glass. She looked as though she was the assistant at a magic show and had just been sawed in half. All she was missing was a slightly skimpier outfit and a sparkly hat.

"I'm just a bit weirded out by Voodoo. I just don't know much about it."

"Well, let's go in and find out. Come on. Don't leave me standing out here."

Exhaling audibly, she took her keys out of the ignition, still feeling unsure about their plans. She had to wait for a car to pass her on the street before she could open the door and join Candy on the sidewalk.

The shop was small. It was on one of the major streets just off of Bourbon Street, a major tourist destination. This well-known street was frequented by travelers from across the globe. It harbored several bars, night clubs, music venues, and homeless people. The greatest draw, Mardi Gras, took place in the Springtime, annually. Although based on a Catholic holiday, God seemed to be very far away from the minds of Mardi Gras goers. Mardi Gras usually featured parades with decorated floats, that were filled with drunk people, who were throwing plastic beads at other drunk people, many who were flashing their breasts. It wasn't exactly Sunday school. There were some family friendly versions, but many people went to downtown parades for one reason, to party. Mardi Gras parades were one party scene where Hazel put her foot down. She despised them. When Mardi Gras came, she stayed as far away from the festivities as she could.

She surveyed the outside of the shop with hesitation. Its peeling dark green shutters with icicle Christmas lights in July weren't exactly throwing off a vibe that made her think of a place of business she longed to enter. The building's exterior had blotches of burnt orange and white paint, so she didn't know what look the owner was initially going for, but she didn't think they had achieved it.

She walked in the door, hoping to make a quiet entrance, but the bell above the door chimed as the door swung open, squashing her plan. The smell of different incense filled her nostrils. She couldn't place the specific fragrances but figured it was a special blend.

A middle-aged woman came out of a curtained off back room. She had on a red, African style top with a matching headscarf. Her face had white blotches of what could only be described as war paint. She wore huge gold-hooped earrings, and carried a large Voodoo style doll that had a wooden African mask for a head. She cringed at how creepy the doll was.

"Good afternoon, cher. What brings the two of you in today?" the woman asked, while fixing the clothing on the doll hanging from her arm. The Cajun dialect surprised Hazel.

"It's just me. I'm just browsing." Hazel responded.

"If you say so, cher. Let me know if you need some help."

The woman moved behind the glass counter and busied herself with the display.

Hazel felt uneasy. She began looking through random trinkets on the shelves, pretending to be shopping.

No square inch of the shop was bare. It was

covered with dolls, charms, beads, and odd artifacts. There were also several African style masks and instruments. There was so much to look at, it made her dizzy. She could have sworn that the eyes of some dolls followed her as she walked. She caught herself checking over her shoulder more times than was probably warranted, but the entire store gave her the creeps. Considering what she did for a living with the spirit world, the irony wasn't lost on her.

As she moved through the small shop, she couldn't help but notice that the woman had not only been watching her, but also watching Candy. She had to know if the woman could see spirits, so she walked back over to the glass counter.

"Excuse me."

"I knew that you'd come back for help, cher. What can I help you with?"

"When I first came in, I couldn't help but notice you welcomed the two of us. Who were you referring to?"

The woman smiled and nodded her head.

"Ah, yes. I was referring to you and your red-headed friend, my child. Certainly, you didn't think you were the only one who could see her?"

Hazel felt slightly embarrassed.

"No, ma'am, it's just that, besides my mother and grandmother, I've never met anyone else who could."

"Well, I am glad to further open your eyes, my child. What is it that brings you into my store today? Having trouble with the spirit world? Or maybe the world of the living? Maybe someone in your life has done you wrong?"

"Definitely not the second one. I'm having an issue with spirits appearing to me in my apartment. I wondered if there was a way to keep my personal space, well, personal?"

"I can give you ways to rid yourself of evil, but not to rid yourself of spirits who are not. If I did that, it would also act to keep out your red-headed friend."

"Candy..."

"Right, Candy, and I doubt you would want to keep her out. You can take this dried sage, though, just in case you need it one day."

The woman handed her a bundle of dried sage that was tied with a string.

"You can burn this in your apartment and let the smoke infiltrate the crevices where dark energies could linger. It should drive them out. If it doesn't, we can look at more extreme options. It will drive out the dark, but it won't drive out the light."

"Okay, thank you so much. How much do I owe you?"

"I don't need any of your money for the sage. Just keep on your current path and the rewards will be payment enough. Take care now, cher."

"Um, okay. You too."

She walked out, more confused than when she arrived. Was the woman talking about continuing her path in defending Roy? Or her path in helping Angela? If so, how did she know that? How did this perfect stranger know details about her life? Had she just encountered someone who was psychic? She had left with so many questions. She tucked the sage into her bag, got into her car, and headed home.

"So, are we going to use it, then?"

"Use what?"

"The sage, silly."

"Oh, I hadn't actually thought about it. I'm not sure if I should burn anything in the apartment. I'll probably just hang onto it for now. I mean, she said that it cleans out evil, and that isn't our problem, anyway. I don't want to set off the smoke alarms."

"Yea, that makes sense. What did you think about that store? And that woman?"

"I don't know what to think."

"Yea."

* * *

After leaving the Voodoo shop, she and Candy went back to their apartment so she could get cleaned up and change for her interview with Raymond Waters. It was the one day when she wanted to look professional, and be on time.

When she arrived at Raymond's Garden District mansion at 4:30 p.m., it was clear they were setting up for a big event. Catering vans were blocking part of the street, and bartenders, dressed in tuxedos, were shining wine glasses at the bar. Mr. Waters met her at the door and brought her down to his office. He offered her a brandy and then sat down at the large mahogany desk that was directly across from her. The room was large and in the shape of an oval, but it was filled with equally robust pieces of furniture and antique decor, with a European theme throughout. Raymond Waters was no stranger to spending his money. He seemed to have a relaxed way about him, which she attributed to his confidence.

His home was in the heart of the Garden District and would have been built before the turn of the century. It was the type of home one would have seen symphonies hosted in during the early 1900s. It had large living spaces, grand staircases, original inlaid floors, soaring ceilings, historical fireplaces and ornate doors. In an impoverished city, this was the house of a multimillionaire. This man had a lot to lose.

She had never met Raymond Waters; however, she had seen him on television ads and billboards. His family business had run through many generations before him. He was definitely what one would call 'Old Money' in the deep south of Louisiana. In a place like South Louisiana, a family like his wielded a lot of power. It was his power she was afraid of.

Although in his mid-fifties, Mr. Waters was a handsome man. With salt and pepper hair and a matching beard, he looked very distinguished. His dark eyes made her feel like she was looking into black holes; she found it hard to look away. Since the death of his wife years prior, he appeared to be New Orleans' most eligible bachelor. She doubted he had any issues with finding women to date. He walked with an air of confidence that only wealth and success could create. If he did kill someone, he certainly wasn't concerned with getting caught. Sadly, men like him rarely had to pay for their crimes, and he knew that.

"So, what brings you here to speak with me tonight, Miss Watson, is it?" Raymond asked casually, while topping off his glass. He leaned back in his posh leather chair and propped his shined dress shoes onto the desk. She wished she felt as relaxed as he did, instead of feeling like she needed to vomit, since the sensation had grown as he spoke. She did her best to hide her nausea and appear tougher than she felt.

"I am the public defender for Roy Miller. I just wanted to ask you a few questions."

"Oh. I took a chance on him right of out college. I knew his family came from nothing, therefore he was very motivated to prove something to himself. It's just so unfortunate that he got himself into so much trouble. I had high hopes for him; I thought his motivation would get him far."

"So, do you honestly believe that Roy committed those crimes? You don't suspect it could have possibly been someone else?"

She wondered if she had probed too hard, as Mr. Waters seemed taken aback by her question. He dropped his feet back onto the floor and placed his elbows on the desk. His jaw tightened.

"Who do you suggest it could have been, Miss Watson? Roy was in charge of my books. It was Roy or me, and it wasn't me. Unless that is what you are insinuating."

"I'm not insinuating anything, sir. I'm just

trying to defend my client and I can't do that properly unless I understand the whole story. They recently announced, on the news, that Roy's former coworker, Angela Spencer, has gone missing. Her disappearance and your company's embezzlement situation could be related. I'm trying to understand how Roy fits into all of this."

"Are you an attorney for her family, Miss Watson?"

"No, I am not. Again, I am trying to help Roy and I'm here for that purpose. However, what happened to Angela could be relevant to Roy's case, so I needed to ask."

"Well, I am sure Angela's whereabouts and Roy's crimes are unrelated, and therefore her situation is none of your business. I have guests coming, Miss Watson, and frankly, I don't like where this conversation is going. I'm going to have to ask you to leave."

Mr. Waters pushed his chair away from the desk and she shifted uncomfortably in her seat. The interview had gotten away from her.

"With all due respect, Mr. Waters, I'm not

trying to accuse you of anything. I'm only trying to help Roy, and Angela, if I can. I hoped you would be willing to assist."

"Angela used to work for me, but she no longer does. That's all I can tell you about her. Roy committed crimes against my company. Now, if you don't mind, I have guests to attend to. Goodbye, Miss Watson."

She stood up to leave Mr. Waters' office, but he met her around the front of his desk before she had a chance to exit the room. Moving in uncomfortably close to her face, he breathed a sickening breath into her neck. She felt as though he was a caged lion and she was his prey. She had made a mistake going there to meet with him, going without Candy there to support her. She desperately wanted to leave. Over his shoulder, she could see Angela manifesting next to a large mahogany armoire. She closed her eyes and pleaded for Angela to help her, but no help came. And then, he spoke.

"I am a powerful man, Miss Watson. And I know a lot of formidable people in this town, in a lot of high places. Wherever you are going with this, I suggest you stop, if you know what is good for you."

He threw the door open on his way out of the room. She was much too shaken to stay in his home any longer. She knew Angela needed her help, but Angela would have to wait, so she made a promise to her, hoping that her words hadn't fallen on deaf ears.

She grabbed her bag and ran out of the house as fast as she could. She could not hold back the downpour of tears that had started to fall, matching those that threatened to fall from the sky. If she was going to get anything out of Waters, it would not be out of him willingly, and she would not stick around to try.

She made it back to her apartment quicker than she thought was even possible. Candy immediately wrapped her in a towel and helped her get into dry clothes. The storm started as soon as she got into her car, so she had gotten drenched from the rain. Candy fixed her a cup of tea before setting her down on the sofa. As far as spirits went, Candy was as helpful as they came, at least when she wanted to be.

"I really don't know how Angela expects me to solve her murder if she won't give me anything to go on. She's so damn cryptic! I know Raymond killed her. I just need proof. I have to get back into his house so I can look around when he isn't there. Angela was there for a reason. She showed up in his office. There's something there. There's definitely more to the story between them."

"Hazel, you cannot go breaking into that man's house! It almost certainly has impenetrable high-tech security, not to mention he's most likely a damn murderer! It's too dangerous. You said you would only ask him a few questions and then you'd stand back and let the police do their job. I don't want you to end up like me. You're not invincible! This has gone too far."

Candy's form flickered as spectral tears fell from her eyes, purely out of distress, but Hazel was undeterred. She knew Waters was the perpetrator in the embezzlement, and in Angela's murder, so she was insistent on proving it, no matter the stakes. And since she knew

Tate would not approve, she had no intention of telling him. It was another thing she would have to wrestle with in her mind later.

"He's hiding something, Candy. I just know it. You can help me. I won't go without you again. You can be my lookout. We are a team. I'm not helpless. We can be safe. Plus, he's so full of himself that I doubt he thinks he'll ever get caught."

"I still don't like it, Hazel. I don't like it at all. You don't know what he's capable of."

8

The
Break-in
and the
Abduction

Before testing her luck in trying to get into Raymond Waters' home, she did as Tate suggested and made photocopies of the documents Angela had hidden at her mother's home. She knew she couldn't put it off any longer. The police needed that paperwork if she wanted Raymond to get caught. She added an anonymous letter stating that Raymond Waters was behind Angela's disappearance and the embezzlement of his company. She dropped off one copy in the mail delivery box at the police station, addressed to the police chief. Another copy went into the mail to the FBI. She didn't know who to address it to, so she went through the main website and chose the best address and contact person she could find. She didn't have any control over what happened to the paperwork once it left her, which was concerning. Hopefully, the packages made it into the right hands, but all she could do was hope. She kept her own copy hidden beneath her mattress.

She and Candy climbed into her sedan and headed to the Garden District, Waters' part of the city. She hoped to get into his house, find something incriminating, and get out quickly, with him being none the wiser. That was her plan, although her plans rarely worked out as she intended them to. His wife had died years prior, and he had no children, so the house should have been empty, as long as there were no housekeepers there. That was one factor she hoped would not change, because she didn't want to have to return another day, just because someone was in the house. She really needed to get this over with, while she still had her nerve. If she had to sleep on it, she would probably change her mind about breaking into Raymond's home. Not only was it dangerous, but it was against the law. She rolled her eyes thinking about the trouble she was getting herself into, but she moved forward anyway.

"I just need for you to watch Raymond while I'm in his house. He should be at work until about 5. Let me know when he leaves work and I'll get out of there before he has any clue that someone was inside."

"Alright, but be careful! If you hear or see anyone, you need to get the hell out of there!"

"I will. I promise."

Candy left Hazel's side to go to Waters' office, while Hazel drove to his house, arriving before 3 and parking her car among the others on the side of his street. The tree-lined streets of the Garden District had lots of shrubbery and flowering plants, which allowed her to get into his backyard without being seen, at least she hoped she hadn't been seen. She moved quickly, just to be sure.

Raymond Waters' backyard looked like something out of a Home and Gardens magazine. Although small, as expected in downtown New Orleans, everything was lush and in bloom. A large oak tree stood in the center of the yard, giving shade to a beautifully carved gazebo. There were roses, gardenias, and azalea bushes, all full of beautiful white and pastel flowers. An exquisite granite water fountain stood off to the side, carved in a Romanesque style. It was an unexpectedly serene setting for such an evil man, which was incredibly ironic.

When she got to Raymond Waters' back door, she looked around for a spare key and found one beneath one of the several potted plants on the back porch. Nerves aside, she quietly made her way inside. Dropping beside the large kitchen island, she sat quietly for a few minutes, listening for signs that anyone else was in the house, but the house was eerily silent.

As she was looking around the vast marble island in the center of the kitchen, she could see Angela's spirit walking down the hall and into Waters' office, where she had been only days earlier. Believing she was alone in the house, Hazel stood back up and made her way down the hall and into the office, in an effort to follow the wayward spirit. The closer she got to Angela, the stronger the barrage of Angela's emotions became. Hazel closed her eyes, doing her best to build up her protective walls, before moving in closer to the spirit.

Angela was standing in front of the armoire, fiddling with her sapphire necklace, and staring longingly at the bulky piece of furniture. As it had in the past, the necklace flickered with Angela's touch, as though she were flipping a light switch as she rubbed it. Not suspecting that Angela was going to speak to her, Hazel started opening the drawers of the armoire and going through each drawer's contents. Clearly, there was something in them she needed to find, but the giant piece of furniture was filled to the max with a variety of items. Files, airline ticket stubs, keys, and pictures cluttered what seemed to be all junk drawers. It was a lot to go through. She looked at Angela desperately, holding up her hands to say that she didn't know what else to do. She needed Angela's help. Finally, Angela came closer to her, and pointed at the third drawer. Hazel's heartbeat started beating faster, making her slightly dizzy, but she took a deep breath, slowly released it, and focused in on Angela.

Relieved that Angela finally appeared to want to help her, she opened the drawer that Angela was zeroed in on and pulled everything out. She saw nothing worth the cryptic drama that Angela deemed appropriate, but she slowed down her rummaging to make sure that she missed nothing. Then, as she thought she had seen everything in the drawer, she noticed that the wood in the back of the drawer did not match the rest of it. She pushed on the discolored piece, and it gave way to another compartment behind a false back. Inside of the false back was a small, black, velvet bag. The bag had a surprising weight to it, so she gently untied the string holding it closed and poured the contents into her hand. The item that fell out of the bag was Angela's Star Sapphire necklace. A rush of energy filled her, sending a tingling sensation through her arms and legs, but the feeling was violently halted by a feeling of intense dread. She had to get out of there immediately. Shocked at her discovery and desperate to get out of the house of a murderer, she quickly slipped the necklace into the pocket of her pants. Turning around to leave, she caught a flash of Raymond Waters, felt a sharp pain on the side of her head, and then she fell into darkness.

* * *

Hazel didn't know how long she had been unconscious when she woke up in the trunk of a car. Her hands and feet were bound, and her eyes were blindfolded. All she could see was darkness. All she could hear were the sounds of the road, the sounds of which led her to believe that the road was not paved because of how aggressively the car bounced around on its tires. It took all of her strength just to stop her head from being banged against the roof of the trunk. Feeling her adrenaline begin to surge, she started to kick and scream frantically, but she was alone. No one was there to hear her, or to set her free, so the car kept on steadily. She had never felt so alone.

After several long minutes of panic, she felt the temperature in the trunk change, and she could sense the calming energy of Candy inside of the trunk with her.

"Hazel, are you okay?" Candy whispered, from somewhere in the darkness.

Hazel tried to lift her head, but a throbbing pain forced her to drop it back down and squeeze her eyes shut. She felt instantly lightheaded. Candy moved in closer and cradled Hazel's head. She struggled but managed to remove the blindfold from Hazel's eyes.

"I'm not sure. Where am I? What happened?" Hazel whimpered, nuzzling her face into Candy's hair.

"I tried to get to you in time! I watched Waters until he left for work, but Angela blocked me when I was getting close to the house! She wouldn't let me go! She wanted Raymond to find you. I don't know why. I tried to get free of her, but everything moved so fast. I'm so sorry, doll. I'm so sorry," Candy sobbed. "By the time she let me go past, Waters had you thrown over his shoulder and had dropped you into his trunk. As far as where you are headed, I'm not sure, but this road isn't paved, and there are trees and swamp everywhere. What did you find in his house?"

Candy began gently petting Hazel's hair to comfort her, but it did not calm her.

"I found Angela's necklace. I think he hit me in the head. My head is killing me, but I can't really remember anything after finding it."

Hazel cried as the realization hit her as to how much trouble she was in, and she started to panic more than she had already been.

Candy pulled her head forward to examine it and then cradled her again.

"You're going to be okay, love. He definitely

hit you on the head. I'm going to get you out of this. I promise."

"He killed her, Candy, so I don't know what that means for my chances of survival."

Her voice hitched as her sobbing increased. She began struggling against her bindings as tears clouded her already closed eyes. Candy tried to help her, but it was no use, they were too tight. She didn't have any room to maneuver her body, and it felt hard to breathe. Her mind raced, thinking about all the horrible fates that may await her at the end of the road.

"Don't say that! I'll get you out of this, doll. I have to leave you for now, though, so that I can go for help."

Hazel reached around to hold Candy tighter, burying her face against her, ignoring the chill of Candy's form.

"Please don't leave me alone in here! You're a spirit, Candy, Tate can't even see you! I can't breathe. Please stay with me," Hazel pleaded helplessly, trying to catch her breath.

"I have to try, love. I'm going to find Tate and try to give him a message through his police scanner. You know I've tried it before. I'll write it on his damn car window if I have to! I'll tell him where you are. Just don't fight Raymond. Don't even speak to him. Do everything you can to stay alive until I get back! I love you! We are in this together!"

"Hurry, please."

She fought back sobs as Candy hugged her and left her alone in the darkness again.

Her mind raced as the car slowed down to a stop. Too exhausted to fight, she was destined to find out just how Angela had felt in her last moments, and she was resigned to accept the same fate. She thought of her family, Tate, and Candy, and was furious at herself for not listening to them when they warned her to leave the investigation alone. Although she knew that Raymond Waters was dangerous, she had let a ghost haul her into a precarious situation that was going to get her killed anyway. Her thoughts even went to Roy, and how she was going to let him down. She was so close to getting to the truth, and proving his innocence, and then she had to make a stupid mistake, and get herself abducted. If she wouldn't have been so terrified, she would have gone further down a shame spiral. The reality of the situation pulled her out of it, before she sunk in too deep.

As the trunk opened, she felt she had a little more fight in her, although it was all in vain. She screamed, but in taking in her surroundings, she realized he had brought her to the middle of the swamp, so there was no one who would hear her. The scene was just like she had seen in her nightmares so many times before, and it made her heart sink. Forgetting her temporary handicap, she tried to run, but her leg bindings caused her to fall face down in the mud. The throbbing in her head was excruciating. Before she even knew what was happening, unconsciousness came upon her again.

* * *

Hazel awoke to the sound of voices. It sounded like a distant mumbled whisper. She could hear a few of them, but she struggled to make out any of the words. Her head still throbbed from where Raymond had hit her. She pulled against the bindings on her hands one more time, but they were still too tight, so she tried to focus on the voices again.

"Oh, no."

"It's happened again."

"We need to save her!"

They continued to plead with each other, but they didn't seem to realize she could hear them.

"Hello," she cried, "Help me."

She struggled against the floor, trying to right herself. She expected to see a room full of women. It sounded like there were several of them talking in the background. Instead, what she saw shocked her, making her shudder. She was in some sort of rustic cabin, surrounded by three female spirits. Two of them stared down at her with the look of horror on their faces.

One lady was blond, similar to Angela. She looked to be about forty years old and was dressed in Western attire, with cowboy boots and a hat. Her hair was feathered around her face. The youngest of the women was very young, maybe eighteen. She stayed towards the corner so Hazel couldn't make out a lot of her features, although she could see her eyes were wide with fear. The last woman was sitting in a chair and looking out of the window. Hazel could see her there, but the woman did not acknowledge her. From where the woman was sitting, Hazel could not see any more details about her.

"Can you see us?" the blond spirit asked.

"Yes, I can. Where am I? Why are all of you here?"

"We are stuck here, love. Well, we aren't stuck here, but we mostly stay here, because we are all buried on this property. He killed us here. This is his cabin. What is your name? How did you get mixed up with that monster? Oh, and my name is Sheila, by the way."

Hazel felt sick to her stomach and she was forced to turn her face to the side and retch. Raymond was a serial killer. What were the odds that she had gotten herself mixed up with a man like that?

Heaving and trying to catch her breath, Hazel sat herself back upright.

"My name is Hazel. I was digging into a missing woman's case. Her name is Angela

Spencer. Her spirit led me to believe that Raymond may have had something to do with her disappearance, therefore I broke into his house when he was at work. I know it was reckless, but the spirit of Angela would not stop trying to lead me to something. Just as I started finding the evidence I was looking for, Raymond found me in his house. He must have hit me over the head with something, because I don't remember anything, until I woke up in his trunk. Do you ladies know Angela?" she asked with a trembling voice.

The younger lady stepped forward and interrupted: "My name is Danielle Carter. If you make it out of here, please tell the police and my family where we are so we can finally find peace. I don't want to be here anymore. I want to go home."

After she finished her plea, Danielle went back into the corner. Hazel realized that Danielle may have been afraid of her, which was heartbreaking.

"I would, but I don't know if I'm going to make it out of here alive. A friend of mine was going to try to notify the police of my situation, but she is like you, so I'm not sure if he will get her message. Most people cannot see spirits like I can."

Sheila walked past her and looked out of the window.

"We have seen her here before, Angela, that is. He brought her here, and she met the same fate as we did. She doesn't stay around, however. She comes and goes. She doesn't come into the cabin. She usually stays out there by that tree," she said.

Hazel stepped on her tiptoes so she could peek out of the window. Angela was out there, just as Sheila had stated, sitting on a tree stump. The scene was just as she had seen it in Angela's memories, but through her own eyes. She had always thought she was seeing Angela's memories from before she died, but she felt a sick sense of trepidation at realizing it was possibly Angela's memories of the swamp as a spirit that she had been seeing in her nightmares. She thought, perhaps, that Angela may have never set living eyes on that swamp at all.

Danielle approached her again, appearing to be at last feeling a little safer talking to her.

"We will do our best to protect you until the police find you. If they find you, then they will find us," Danielle said.

"That would be the best-case scenario, but how will you do that? How will you stop him? I doubt he will leave me here alone for long. I don't even have a weapon. I can't fight him," Hazel said, as she felt her tears return.

"We have a few powers, dear. Some of us have been here for a long time. We look forward to the chance to scare the shit out of that bastard." Sheila flashed a devilish grin.

"For now, Hazel, we need to get your hands and feet unbound. Keep pulling at your bindings, and we will look around for something to help you. We don't know when he will be back, but when he returns, you need to be ready to fight for your life."

She did as she was told, pulling at her feet first, and getting them separated with the help of Sheila. Then she could stand up and walk around looking for a way to untie her hands.

She was able to break a small but sharp piece of wood from the baseboard trim and carefully used it to saw away the binding that was on her hands. After her hands were free, she slid the piece of wood into her waistband, in case she needed to use it as a weapon later. With the help and support of the other women, she felt a small glimmer of hope at the possibility of rescue.

"Hazel, there isn't a way to get out of this cabin until he comes back and opens the door. We've all tried, and we all failed. All the bolt locks require a key and there are bars on all the windows. All you can do now is wait to bombard him when he comes back," said Sheila.

All three of the women looked troubled. She suddenly felt crushed again. She was a sitting duck. She was stuck in that cabin unless she starved to death, Raymond came back and killed her or, by the smallest chance, someone rescued her. Her odds weren't good at all, and she felt it.

"Since we have some time to sit and wait, do y'all want to tell me a little about how you all got here. I need something to keep my mind busy," she asked, as she found a place on the floor to sit, leaning up against the wall.

Sheila sat down next to her and began her story. "I'm from Houston, Texas. I met Raymond at a Honkey Tonk club, and we hit it off right away. We danced together for hours. He seemed like a catch, so when he asked if I'd like to go with him for coffee, I enthusiastically accepted. We got into his BMW, but instead of going to a coffee shop, he parked the car in an alley in the absolute worst part of the city. I immediately got scared and started trying to get out of the car, but I couldn't because he had the child locks on. I screamed as he raped me and that's all I remember. Somehow, I ended up in this cabin. Danielle was already here when I arrived, as was Laurie, the dark-haired lady who has been sitting over in that chair since you got here. All we know about Laurie is her name. We haven't been able to find out anything else about her."

"Laurie... that name sounds familiar."

Hazel dug around in her brain to fish out where she knew the name from.

"Laurie, that's Raymond's late wife's name," Hazel said as the realization hit her.

Her statement caused Sheila and Danielle's jaws to drop. She gently walked over to the lady by the name of Laurie and sat beside her.

"Laurie, is it? Were you Raymond's wife?"

Laurie glanced over into Hazel's eyes, and then she turned away.

"I'm sorry to pry, Mrs. Laurie. I'm just afraid and trying to understand why all of you are here. Are you Raymond's wife?"

Laurie pulled her legs over to sit in more of a sideways position until she was facing Hazel. She was a beautiful woman. Hazel could definitely imagine her being Raymond Waters' type of lady and, based on the clothes she was wearing, it was also obvious she was wealthy in life. You could tell she died quite young, maybe in her late thirties.

"I am Raymond's wife. Well, I was, until he murdered me. He brought me here for 'fresh air.' He told me it would do me some good, then he smothered me while I slept. I watched from this chair while he called 911 to tell them that his wife wasn't breathing. I realized what had happened to me. Because of my cancer, they never pushed for an autopsy and, clearly, he didn't want one. I'm not sure where my body is, but I assume it's in the family plot. I don't know why he did this to me. I guess I had become too much of a burden, so he wanted to move onto the next best thing. I can't imagine going back to my house and having to see him, so I stay here. I want to move on, but not until I get justice, not until Raymond pays for what he's done to me, to all of us."

"My gosh, Laurie, I'm so sorry for what happened to you. He is such a monster! How has he gotten away with this for so long?" Hazel cried.

Danielle moved in closer and also sat next to Laurie.

"I believe she was his first, or at least she was the first to end up here. I met Raymond when I was walking home from school during my senior year. He offered to give me a ride home. He was clearly a high-class man since he drove such a nice car so I just didn't think he could be a dangerous man. It was naïve of me, for sure. He held a gun to my head and drove me here. He kept me locked up here for months. I was scared and starved. I prayed for rescue that never came. Eventually, he got tired of having to deal with me, so he ended it. I've been here ever since. I saw what he did to you, Sheila. I wished I could have stopped him. I'm so sorry." Danielle said as her tears brought them out of everyone.

When Danielle was finished talking about what Raymond had done to her, Hazel felt the need for fresh air, but the most she could do was to go to the window. She slowly stood up and peaked through the bars on the windows. She could see Angela, still sitting on the tree stump, and looking out over the water, but Angela was shaking, and appeared to be crying.

"She does that a lot." stated Sheila. "He buried her here. I think she knows that. She never speaks to us, so we don't have a lot of information. I think she is confused about her death. She may not even realize she is dead. We try to get her attention; we try to talk to her, but I'm starting to think she is too scared to talk to us. Maybe she thinks it would make her situation more real."

"She's been appearing to me for weeks. She's very cryptic, so I've had to go well out of my way to find out anything about her situation. I realized Raymond killed her but, for some reason, she wanted Raymond to find me in his house. I usually have a spirit with me. Her name is Candy. She is my best friend, my back-up no matter what. She tried to warn me that Raymond was close to getting home, so I could get out of there, but Angela prevented her from warning me. I don't understand why she would endanger me like that. I'm guessing she did that in hopes of her body being found if they ever found me, but I still don't understand the thought process of putting my life in danger when she was already dead. There is no way to bring her back. I wish there was, but there isn't."

She wiped a stray tear from her eye. She felt more flustered than she did when she first spoke to Candy about what Angela had done back at the house. She knew Raymond needed to be caught before he could kill more women, but she would really prefer not to be sacrificed in the process.

At some point in the night, Hazel had fallen asleep. She didn't know how long she had been there, in that old cabin in the swamp, all she knew was that day had turned to night, and her exhaustion had eventually overtaken her fight to stay awake. She awoke to find Candy, having just gotten back from trying to find help, gently petting her hair. Even with the calming energy that Candy brought to her, she still awoke with a jolt, not recognizing her surroundings, and thinking that she was still in one of her many nightmares.

"I think I got the message to Tate. He realizes you are missing because you missed court today. When I left him, he was looking into Raymond Waters' properties and trying to find out Raymond's whereabouts today," Candy said exasperated. "But we have a problem. I think Raymond knows the cops are onto him and he's heading this way. I think he plans to get rid of the evidence. We need to come up with a plan to keep you safe until the police can find you."

"What can we possibly do? We can't keep him out indefinitely. I'm stuck in here."

She found it hard to think straight. She was feeling her cortisol levels rise as the fight-or-flight sensation surged through her. She wanted the flight, but she had no way to get out of the godforsaken cabin!

Laurie stood up for the first time since Raymond had brought Hazel to the cabin.

"Just because he has the keys doesn't mean we can't try to keep him out. We can reinforce the doors and windows with the furniture. We can try to hold him off. It's our only chance to buy Hazel time until the police get here," Laurie said as she moved towards the door.

Hazel got to work and, with the help of the ladies' spirit energies, flipped the sofa onto its side and pushed it up against the front door. The ladies had a lot more spectral power than she had expected. The bathroom only had a small window with bars on it. She could climb through it if there were no bars, but at least it wasn't big enough for Raymond to get inside if he took the bars off. She locked the bathroom door and pushed the vanity up against it. Candy stayed inside of the bathroom with her, not only to comfort her, but also to offer her immense spectral energy if Raymond showed up at the bathroom door, intent on knocking it down. The other ladies stayed outside of the bathroom so they could use their energy to prevent him from getting inside and attacking him if he did. They had a plan. She just needed to survive until the police found her.

Just as she thought her heart couldn't race any faster, she heard a car speed up, breaks screech, and a door slam. Her heart dropped into her stomach, as the familiar sensation of dread washed over her. She felt like she had stopped breathing, so she began focusing on taking in a breath and making sure to let it out.

Candy grabbed her around her shoulders and sent a chill all over her body.

"He's here, doll, but we've got this. Tate is coming. He will get here soon. We just have to hold Raymond off."

The banging on the door started immediately. Raymond's keys were not working, and he seemed to be getting desperate. He was trying to beat the front door down. She hoped the furniture would hold, but she could only slightly see the front door from the bathroom, so she had no idea if the barricade was still in place. He was frantically beating on the door, and she could hear the ladies screaming instructions to each other as they planned on how to keep him out. Whatever they were doing, it seemed to be working.

Suddenly, the beating stopped. She peeked out of the window again, but she didn't see Raymond anywhere. Clearly, his key didn't work, but he wouldn't give up that easily. She didn't feel relieved; she felt scared of what he would do next.

"Where did he go?"

Hazel whimpered as she coward on the floor.

"I'll go check, love. I'll be right back. Just stay low and quiet."

Candy slid out of the bathroom and into the main house. Hazel could hear their whispers.

She sat quietly on the bathroom floor, drawing shapes into the dust by her feet, while waiting on news from Candy as to where Raymond had gone. She found herself counting floor tiles while trying to calm down her breathing. She no longer felt the need to cry, all she felt was numbness and resolve. Suddenly, the ladies screamed, and Candy flew back into the bathroom, which made Hazel jump.

"Hazel, Raymond was in the shed out back. He was getting a chainsaw. I think he's going to cut his way into the house."

Chills ran down Hazel's entire body.

"Candy, I'm scared. I'm trapped. What am I supposed to do?"

"We won't give up, doll. Don't you give up yet. Tate will get here. The cops will come. Until then, we have your back. Raymond will be in a world of hurt if he walks into this cabin. The ladies are ready to throw every ounce of energy that they have at him. Just you watch. He'd better be ready to go up against some serious poltergeist action!"

The other women had a plan, but she didn't

feel much better. Although she would have liked to be a fly on the wall when Raymond had to go face to face with three angry poltergeists, she would rather not have to face his wrath afterwards. She began regretting so many things about her life. Why didn't she ever give Tate the date he had always asked for, even if he was perhaps joking? Why not even try? Why didn't she see her family enough? Why didn't she have more fun? She spent so much of her life being a mess, instead of taking the time to organize things in a way to help herself prosper. She thought about how she would do so many things differently if she had that one more chance everybody talks about.

Candy grabbed her by the shoulders and shook her.

"Don't you give up on me, Hazel. You hear me. We are going to fight!"

"Wouldn't his time be better spent fleeing the city, or the country, instead of trying to get rid of me?"

The sound of the chainsaw pulled her right out of her self-regret. The house shook as

Waters attempted to cut a hole clean through the exterior wall.

Everything happened so fast. She heard a loud bang and then Danielle, Laurie, and Sheila started screaming and she could hear objects being thrown around the room. Raymond was definitely getting hit by projectiles, as the ladies in the other room were fiercely trying to protect her, and to take Raymond out. She had no doubt that their poltergeist energy was on full display. She wondered why Raymond hadn't turned and run away at the odd sight that it must have been. Most people would have. It told her just how important his money and power were to him. She leaned up against the vanity as Candy wrapped her in a cool embrace. Being so close to a spirit was freezing, but the pressure of Candy's energy made her feel safer. Suddenly, loud bangs started against the bathroom door. She tried to stay quiet, but it took everything she had in her to control her breathing. Who was she kidding? He knew she was in there. Eventually, he would make his way in. He was ramming the door with his shoulder, and she didn't have the strength to hold him off.

After only about ten minutes of struggling, Raymond pushed the door open. She scurried to the corner and braced herself. Paralyzed with fear, she could do nothing else. Anger was etched across his face, and his lips were curled into a snarl. He was bloodied and bruised, especially on his face. His victims had taken out all that they had on him, and it showed. She wondered what he must have been thinking as projectiles flew at his face. Did he know that the spirits of his victims were taking their revenge? She guessed she would never know. Raymond lunged at her, straddling on top of her and wrapping his fingers around her neck. She struggled against his firm grip, digging her fingernails into his wrists, trying to dislodge him. His eyes held a certain fury, but he never spoke to her; he only grunted words she couldn't make out. If he was speaking, she didn't hear him. Maybe it was because her senses were in overdrive, or maybe it was because she was screaming silently, continuously trying to pry his fingers away, but slowly losing consciousness. Candy jumped onto his back and tried to pry him off of her, but Candy's energy was waning. After using up so much of her energy throughout the day, Candy's form was fading in and out of materialization. Hazel, remembering that she had put the sharp piece of trim into her waistband, started struggling to free her hand so she could get at her makeshift weapon, while still using the other hand to protect her neck from Raymond. In one swift movement, she reached for the shank that was in her waistband and plunged it into Raymond's neck. Raymond, caught by surprise, released her, started sputtering blood, and rolled onto the floor into a crumpled heap. As she watched him bleed out, his victims crowded around him and cursed their goodbyes.

Suddenly, as her head pounded, it hit her just how tired she was. She needed to rest, if only for a minute. She stumbled over to the tattered couch in the living area and peered around at the destroyed cabin. There was a large hole in the wall where Raymond had taken a chainsaw to the building. There were broken dishes and decor laying in bits across the floor. She didn't know how her new friends had caused all the damage to the cabin and to Raymond, but she was forever indebted to them. She closed her eyes, and she drifted off into darkness.

9

The Rescue
and the
Release

Hazel woke to the sound of sirens and the feeling of someone caressing her face. She opened her eyes to see Tate leaning over her. She didn't know how long she had been asleep, but his face was a welcome sight to the usual nightmares she generally woke up to. It took her a moment before she realized where she was, or how she had gotten there. The day's events flooded back to her in short spurts, until she realized she had just killed a man, which caused her heart to drop dramatically into her feet, causing her to nearly vomit. She was now a murderer, and she didn't know how she was going to compartmentalize that, even if it was in self-defense, and even if he deserved it. It didn't matter. He was dead, and she had to live with the fact that she had taken his life. Tate's touch, thankfully, grabbed her attention. She would have to focus on therapy later.

"You're okay, Hazel. I'm here. I've got you. You're going to be okay. Just rest," Tate said.

He cradled her face as her head continued to spin from her head wound and exhaustion. She could see Candy hovering just over his right shoulder. Candy smiled at her and reached out to touch her hand. She tried to sit up but got dizzy. She definitely had a concussion. Tate tried to lay her back down, but she needed to get out of there. The threat may have been over, but her body didn't know that yet. She needed to know what was going on. With Tate's help, she stumbled out of the hole that Raymond had cut through the wall to a scene that looked like a treasure hunt. There were ambulances, police, firefighters and unmarked vehicles. Laurie, Danielle, and Sheila were all outside and watching the men with cadaver dogs, who were going around the property and periodically putting little flags into the ground. Angela, still sitting on the same tree stump, looked as though she was waiting for someone. Hazel walked over and sat next to her. If she disregarded the idea of the unmarked graves, she thought that the swampland could be really beautiful. She took in a satisfying deep breath, filled with the air she expected to no longer be breathing after what had happened to her only hours earlier.

"Angela, why are you still here? What more can I do for you?" she asked, just under her breath.

Angela reached out her hand and pointed to the rose bush near their feet and then Angela finally spoke to her.

"I keep being drawn to this place. I don't

know why. What is happening to me? Why do I keep traveling in circles?"

"Do you realize you are dead? Do you remember what happened to you?"

"I think I always knew. I just didn't want to acknowledge it. I wanted to pretend that I was still locked away somewhere, and that I just needed to be found. And my grandmother's necklace. He took it. I need it back. I was supposed to keep it safe."

Angela reached to the necklace around her neck and stroked the stone with her thumb, but it flickered in and out of existence as it was on her neck. She turned her gaze back down to the rose bush and wiped a tear from her cheek. As they sat there together, a cadaver dog pointed towards the rose bush and a man placed a small flag into the ground.

Angela turned to Hazel with tears in her eyes and smiled.

"I don't think you are lost anymore, Angela, and before Raymond grabbed me, I took back your necklace from his house. I still have it."

She pulled the necklace out of her pocket and

showed it to Angela. The star within the sapphire sparkled in the setting sun, just like it had in her dream. Angela's eyes lit up when she saw it, but when she reached out to touch it, she couldn't. Defeated, she quickly pulled her hand back towards her body and twisted her fingers together against her lap.

"Why can't I touch it?"

"I'm really not sure yet, but you will get this necklace back. I promise. I will hold on to it for you, for now. But I will return it to your body before they lay you to rest, no matter what. I won't let anything happen to it."

"Hazel. Hazel. What are you doing over there?" Tate called after her. "You need to get checked out by the EMTs."

He walked over and scooped her up in his arms, wrapping her in a blanket, and bringing her back over to one of the waiting ambulances. She glanced back to Angela, hoping she knew she intended to return and continue their conversation.

As she sat in the back of the ambulance, while they checked her vital signs and dressed her head wound, she watched the coroner bring out the body bag containing Raymond Waters. In the distance, around the side of the house, she could see Raymond's spirit watching his body being taken away. Hopefully, he would cross over and not follow her home. That was one thought that made her grimace. He was one spirit she would visit a Voodoo priestess to remove.

"Okay, Hazel, you're okay. Let's get you home so you can give your statement. Then you can get some much-needed rest."

"I have one more thing I need to do. It won't take long."

She hopped off of the ambulance and walked back over to Angela. Angela looked up expectedly.

"Angela, you don't have to stay here anymore. If you'd like, I could take you home to your parents. I know they are waiting for you, especially your mom."

"Really? You would do that for me?"

"Absolutely. We have to head back to my apartment first, but we can drive to Mobile tomorrow. Is that okay?"

"That would be amazing."

Sheila, Danielle, and Laurie came and spoke their goodbyes and then Hazel, Angela, and Candy walked back to Tate's police cruiser. She was exhausted and ready to go home, take a shower, eat, and get some rest. There was more to do, and her head ached, but she still felt such a sense of relief at having solved Angela's disappearance. Although she couldn't bring Angela back, it was the best result she could offer.

"Tate, Angela's body was at that cabin and so was her spirit. I asked her to come back with us so I could bring her back to her parents tomorrow. I just wanted to let you know in case you felt anything out of the ordinary."

"So, you're telling me there is a ghost in my car right now?"

"Actually two. Candy is here as well. I told you she's almost always with me."

"This is going to take some getting used to," Tate acknowledged with a shrug of his shoulders. "I still want a date though."

He turned and winked, causing her to flush

uncontrollably, but she simply smiled and didn't bother hiding it from him.

"I think you've earned that."

She smiled and reached over to ruffle his hair. Her head may have felt hazy, but her heart was smiling on the inside, for once.

"Oh, did you receive Candy's message over your police scanner? She said she would use it to tell you where I was."

His smile faded slightly.

"Oh, is that what that was? Yeah, she kind of scared the shit out of me, but I think it got me on the right path. I definitely couldn't ignore it, although I figured my mind was just playing tricks on me."

"I'm sorry she scared you."

"Hey," he said while grabbing her hand, interlacing his fingers in hers, "I appreciate her help in getting you home safe. She can scare me all she needs to if your life is in jeopardy."

After walking up to her apartment and getting comfortable, she had to give her statement to Tate and the other detective. Satisfied with her statement, the detective left, but Tate didn't.

"When I asked you for a date, this wasn't what I had in mind."

He grinned, but she rolled her eyes back at him.

"Well, a little adventure hurt no one. Joking obviously."

She pointed to the bandage on her head and made a sad face.

"Well, I'm definitely too tired to go anywhere tonight, but I would totally be okay with you ordering us some takeout. Oh, and I'll need for you to please redress my head wound tonight as well. It can be our first date, unless you had other plans..."

"Thai food, okay?"

"Thai food is perfect."

* * *

After dinner, he helped her into clean clothes and changed the dressings on her head. Her concussion was still present but had improved substantially. It could have been a lot worse. After getting her all cleaned up, he tucked her into bed. He sat on the side of her bed, with her hands in his, watching her face to make sure she was truly okay.

"Tate..."

"Yea?"

"Can you stay with me? I don't want to be alone."

"I was actually going to ask you if I could. I'll just run to my car and grab the bag of clothes I keep in there, so I can change out of my uniform."

"Thank you."

He squeezed her hand lightly and walked out of the room. She heard the apartment door close behind him as he went down to his car. She felt a flutter of excitement but also immense relief. She always had Candy for support but, no offense to Candy, she really wanted a warm body in bed with her this time. After everything that she had been through, she didn't need to be alone and she always felt safer when he was with her.

When Tate returned from his car, he got himself cleaned up. It was clear, at first, that he didn't know where she wanted him to sleep, but she scooted over to make room for him, so he eventually climbed into the bed right next to her. Chills ran through her body when he moved in close, and she closed her eyes to savor the moment. She worked up the courage to move even closer to him, and then she snuggled up beneath his shoulder. She didn't know if he would be receptive, but he snuck a kiss to the top of her head and wrapped his arm around her. She thought she would melt if she laid next to him much longer.

"You know, Hazel, I thought I was going to lose you today. No more taking risks like that, okay? I don't want to lose you. You're important to me. I didn't know what I was going to do."

She rolled over and rested her arms on his chest, so she could look into his eyes, and she could see the sincerity in them. She had taken unnecessary risks, and she had hurt him. She had scared him. It was selfish to put herself in danger like she did, without letting him know beforehand, so he could at least try to help her. She couldn't do that to him again, and she promised herself that she wouldn't.

She cuddled up closer to him as he lightly rubbed her back. She enjoyed the warmth of his skin and wanted to kiss him so badly, but she was too scared to be rejected. He brushed the hair away from her face so he could look her in the eyes. Cradling her face in his hands, he pulled her lips to his. The scent of his face, the softness of his skin, was intoxicating. He pulled her in closer and, for once in her life, she had no desire to fight the intimacy. At least for that moment, she let her walls come tumbling down. She didn't know how long she had been lost in the kiss but, in that moment, all the self-doubt that had convinced her he was joking about wanting to be with her had melted away. There was no longer doubt. He cared about her. He wanted to be with her. She was good enough.

"I promise. You're not going to lose me," she whispered in his ear, before laying her head back down on his chest and letting his scent overwhelm her.

Tate fell asleep with his arm across her stomach that night, but she stayed up for a little while, just to watch him sleep. He looked so peaceful. She watched his chest rise and fall and noticed the little noises he made when he dreamed. She thought he had never looked so gorgeous as when he was asleep, and she felt like she could sleep next to him every night, if he'd let her. Eventually, she allowed sleep to consume her, but she didn't have any nightmares that night.

* * *

"I can't believe you spent the night next to that beefcake and didn't go all the way!" Candy berated her.

"There's plenty of time for that, grasshopper. Tate stayed behind to make sure I was safe, but my misadventure was definitely not a turn on. We did kiss, so there's that."

"So, are you going to give him a chance after all?"

Candy wiggled her eyebrows comically, as she was known to do.

"When I thought I was going to die, I promised myself that I'd do things better if I got another chance. That includes opening myself up to love. So yes, I'm going to give Tate a chance but, for now, I need to take Angela home and then, hopefully, share some good news with Roy. Are you coming?"

"Well, of course I am. I'm your ride or die, remember?"

"Okay, well I just need to talk to Angela first, and then we will hit the road."

Candy nodded to her, gently touching her arm before leaving the room, so she could give her and Angela some privacy.

She sat down with Angela, hoping she could at last get the complete story of how she ended up dead at the hands of Raymond Waters. Having Angela at her apartment, in order to take her back to her mother's home so she could cross over, was most likely her last opportunity to find out the truth. Angela was sitting on the sofa, seeming to be deep in thought. Hazel hated to disturb the moment, but they had little time, so she took the seat next to her.

"How are you feeling, Angela? Are you ready to go back home?"

"I think so," she responded softly.

"Do you think you feel like telling me what happened between you and Raymond?"

Angela shifted in position so that her legs faced towards Hazel, although her eyes still looked at the floor. Hazel could tell that it was not an easy topic for Angela to talk about. She reached out to where Angela's hand was laying in a gesture of support.

"I understand if it's too painful to talk about."

Angela laid a spectral hand over Hazel's and looked up at her with glassy eyes.

"No, it's okay. I know the story needs to be told. I just needed a moment."

Angela used her free hand to straighten out her dress.

"Had you worked for Raymond for long?"

"For about five years."

Angela wiped a stray tear from her cheek.

"Were you having an affair with him? Sorry for being so forward."

Angela shook her head, still crying.

"No, but that didn't mean Raymond didn't try. I loved my husband and had no interest in having anything with Raymond besides working for him. He got angry, but then I'm sure he just moved on to the next thing. John and I eventually split up, but it was because of his drinking, not because of another man."

"I'm so sorry. I didn't know he was trying to interfere with your marriage. That must have made your work environment difficult."

"He wasn't an amiable man to work for. He put on a front as though he was the nicest man that you could meet, one who would take the shirt off of his back to help the next person, but he was a narcissist. He saw everyone else as being beneath him. He didn't care about anyone but himself, he was just great at pretending otherwise."

"I could definitely see that. How did you know he was embezzling?"

"I handled all of his incoming and outgoing mail and phone calls, as well as all financial documents, including bank statements, that he had to sign. It didn't take long before I noticed numbers weren't matching up, or that money was missing. I kept quiet at first and kept copies of the paperwork. I knew Raymond was powerful, but I didn't know all he was capable of."

"Did he know you were watching him?"

"I think he eventually suspected. I guess it would have been closer to my death when his suspicions were confirmed. I confronted him about a document, just another financial statement that had mismatched numbers from what it should have. He didn't react as you would expect a CEO to react. He got angry and became defensive. It must have been a few days later when he called me to his office and pretended to apologize to me. He asked if he could treat me to dinner so he could explain why the paperwork looked off. Since he signed my paychecks, I felt obligated to hear him out. When I met him at the restaurant, he pulled a gun on me and demanded I get into the trunk of his car. I remember little after that."

Angela was no longer crying. She looked stoic. Hazel presumed that, although talking about her ordeal had been jarring for her, she had accepted it.

"Wow, Angela. I'm so sorry you went through

that. You didn't deserve any of it. You were just doing your job. He was the criminal. He was in the wrong. I know no one can do anything to make this right for you, but I'm just so sorry."

"That's not true, Hazel. You helped me. You showed him justice. I'm sorry I put you in danger, but I had to. I knew he would continue to kill if I didn't. I also knew the police were on to him, so the chances of him killing you were slim. I needed for him to bring you to the cabin so your rescue would take place there, so they would find all of our bodies. There were too many victims to think about, and so many more potential victims to protect. I didn't want you to think that I thought you were disposable. That wasn't it at all."

"Oh no, I understand, Angela. It's okay. You don't have to apologize."

Hazel tried to stifle back tears as she felt her own emotions welling up.

"But you ended his reign of terror, Hazel. Because of you, he will never hurt another woman. And you will free Roy. Poor Roy... he never deserved to be drug into any of this. He is a good man. I wanted to help him so badly, but I just couldn't do anything. It had to be you. I felt lost for a long time, and I didn't know how to communicate with you, and I didn't know what to do. I knew Roy needed help, and I knew Raymond needed to be caught. So, thank you for stepping up and doing all you have done in order to see this through. You've made an enormous difference for so many people."

Angela looked up and smiled. For once, Hazel felt like she understood what Angela had wanted from her and she believed she had accomplished that need. The only thing left to do was to bring Angela home to her parents so they could cross over together. That would be the best happy ending she could give to her.

* * *

The second drive to Mobile proved to be a much better experience. No longer wondering what happened to Angela, or worrying about an innocent man serving a significant prison sentence for something he didn't do, she had so much less weight on her shoulders.

She first stopped at John's house to let him

know Angela's body had been found. She also explained how Angela's boss, Raymond Waters, had killed her to hide the fact that he was stealing from his company. John was heartbroken, as she expected he would be. Although they had supposedly ended on bad terms, it was clear he still very much-loved Angela, and she would be missed. Angela got out of the car and said her own goodbyes to John, although he couldn't have known. Hazel instructed John to go to the coroner's office so he could identify Angela's body, because he would have funeral arrangements to make. Angela's mom was in no shape to handle anything like that anymore.

They arrived in Mobile right around lunchtime, and since she hadn't called first, she hoped Sylvia was home. She knocked on the door and was surprised when Sylvia answered right away.

"Miss Hazel, what a pleasant surprise."

"I came because there were some developments in Angela's case, and I thought it better to tell you and Miss Harriet in person.

May I come in? Has the police chief called you yet?"

"Oh, Miss Hazel, Miss Harriet passed away this morning. I thought you were the coroner coming to pick up her body. But no, I have not yet received a call from the police department."

As she spoke to Sylvia, Angela passed around them, walking down the hall and into one of the back bedrooms.

"Oh no, I'm so sorry. Can we sit down and talk, Sylvia?"

"Of course, Miss Hazel. Let's go into the kitchen."

They went into the kitchen and Sylvia put on a pot of coffee. Pulling out two cups and setting them on the small kitchen table, they sat down together.

"There have been some developments in Angela's case. I don't know how to tell you this, but Angela's body was found. Her boss, Mr. Raymond Waters, murdered her. He was stealing from his company, and she knew. He killed her to cover it up."

"Oh, my god. Miss Hazel. How do you know this?"

"This is going to sound hard to believe, Ms. Sylvia, but I need for you to try. I can see spirits. I didn't know Angela in life. Angela found me and led me here. She led me to her body. Her clues told me that her boss played a part in her death. When I went to his house to look for anything to prove it, although he wasn't home, he showed up, beat, and abducted me. He took me to a cabin in the woods and there were many spirits there, women who he had murdered, including Angela. After a significant struggle, he died, but the police showed up and they found Angela's body. I'm still surprised that I'm alive today. I'm sure they will contact you soon to let you know, but I wanted to let you know first."

Sylvia's mouth hung open like a baby bird waiting for its food, but she had a blank look in her eyes. Hazel had seen that look before, so she wasn't sure if Sylvia had bought her story, or if Sylvia's next words were to throw her out.

Thankfully, Sylvia's next words came as a surprise.

"I believe you, Miss Hazel. I've sensed Mrs. Angela here, and Mr. Earl as well. I just don't know what else to say. This is just so tragic."

"Yes, it is. So, the real reason I came here was to help Angela cross over. I brought her with me so she could cross over with her parents. It was something I needed to do for her so I could help her find peace. She's in the room with her mom. If you don't mind, could we go there right now?"

"Absolutely. Reuniting this family would be a beautiful end to this tragic situation."

They walked down the hall into what appeared to be Mrs. Harriet's room. Harriet was lying on the bed and was clearly deceased. She appeared to have passed away, peacefully, in her sleep. Hazel thought, to herself, that it was a lucky way to go, with no pain or fear. Harriet's spirit, along with Earl's spirit, stood near the window. They looked down at the bed, with worry, as Angela lay there holding her mother's body.

"Angela, I'm so sorry for your loss, but your

parents are waiting for you. You should join them."

Angela looked at her with tear-stained eyes.

"I'm scared."

"Of what?"

"I'm scared of what comes next."

"I know it must be scary. I don't know what comes next. What I know is that when I see people cross over, and they see the other side, they usually smile back at me, if they remember me at all. I don't know what that means, but I don't think it's a bad thing. Plus, I doubt your parents would lead you wrong. You've been stuck here for long enough. You deserve rest."

Angela got up from the bed and walked to join her parents. They embraced each other as they were enveloped in light. It only took a few moments before they faded completely from sight. Hazel felt a tremendous sense of relief when all three of them crossed over into whatever came next. She didn't know what that was, but she didn't think it could be so bad if they had gone there together.

The coroner's van arrived a short while

afterwards, so she quickly said goodbye to Sylvia before leaving to drive back to New Orleans. She made one more stop, however; she had to stop at the prison.

On the walk into the prison that day, she had a bit of a pep in her step. She was finally bringing good news to an innocent man who had suffered long enough. This time, instead of meeting Roy in the conference room, she met with him in the regular visiting area.

"Good afternoon, Miss Hazel. Any news for me today?"

"What would you say if I offered to drive you home?"

"Excuse me, Miss Hazel. What do you mean by drive me home? I'm in prison. I can't just up and leave."

"You can now. Here are your release papers! They have dropped all the charges against you. Raymond Waters took the fall for his own crimes, and he died fighting. You, my friend, are a free man. So, I'll ask you again, do you want me to give you a ride home?"

Roy jumped up from the table and ran around

to wrap her in a hug. The guard shot forward, but she held up her hand to say it was okay. He had tears in his eyes, and she couldn't help but to shed a few herself. After all the worry she had that she wouldn't be a good enough attorney to prevent him from serving time for a crime he didn't commit, she realized she hadn't done too bad.

"Thank you, Miss Hazel. Thank you for believing in me. I owe you my life. Thank you."

"You are truly welcome, Mr. Miller. Now, let's get out of here, before they change their minds."

"Oh, Miss Hazel, can we grab food on the way home? I'm suddenly starving!"

"You got it."

She walked Roy out of prison a free man. She had cleared his name and, for once, she didn't feel like a failure. She had done something good, and she could ride that high into at least the next week, before getting herself into another debacle.

She and Roy listened to music on the way to his mom's house, and she let him choose the radio station. She lowered it just enough so that they could still have a conversation. After having spent weeks in prison, he had a lot to say. His smile never fell once. They stopped at a soup and sandwich shop to pick up enough food for him to bring home lunch for his mother, and brother as well. She had little money to spare, but it was worth it.

Roy invited her in to meet his mother, Irene, who was preparing to go into surgery in the upcoming days. After having grown so close to Roy throughout their ordeal, she agreed, so they visited briefly. Roy's deceased father's spirit, Reginald, had showed up for Roy's release, however he hadn't called the rest of his family to let them know he was getting out of prison early, so everyone was very surprised and crying happy tears when he walked into the door. His mother was a gracious woman who didn't want to let Hazel out of her arms and repeatedly thanked her for helping to bring her boy home. She promised Hazel lots of Sunday brunches with pecan pies, after her surgery recovery of course. Roy could not stop laughing. He couldn't have been happier to be back with his family, and it may have been the first case that ended with Hazel feeling warm and fuzzy. She wasn't from a southern family but she, at least sometimes, wished she was. Southern hospitality was well known for a reason, and Roy's family was the epitome of it. Sitting with them made her think a bit about her own family, and how you realize the important things in life when they are almost taken away. She felt inspired, and she promised herself that she would stop putting off calling her mom. She may need her guidance, after all.

After she dropped Roy off at his family home, she finally felt she had the time to go home and relax, maybe even do a little laundry, but not that night. Tate was waiting at her apartment for her, so her laundry would have to wait. For months, Candy had been tirelessly teasing her about making a move on him so, although her stomach was in knots just thinking about it, she thought she may have the courage to try, especially after all she had accomplished. She had even washed her hair, just in case he got close enough to smell it.

10

The Next Step and Goodbye

A thunderstorm began as soon as she left Roy's mom's house. She didn't let that ruin her mood, however, because she knew Tate's smiling face would be waiting for her when she got home. They had planned to go out but opted to stay in because of the dreadful weather that had been forecast. It was nearly impossible to plan anything in South Louisiana during the summer months, but she was actually looking forward to staying in.

By the time she got out of her car and made it up to her front door, she was drenched.

"This rain is a nightmare!" she sighed, as she sloppily shook the water off of her umbrella.

Tate, who was leaning up against the door frame, had received some of the watery spray from it, but pretended not to notice.

"I know, and it looks like we may get a tropical storm or something within the next week."

He took her umbrella while she fumbled with her keys.

"Damn. Don't tell me that. I don't want to have to evacuate right now."

She got the door open, and they shuffled inside, shutting out the rain and tossing off their wet shoes.

She had forced Candy, after a bit of opposition, to find somewhere else to be that night so she and Tate were, for the first time, alone. Just knowing that made her feel like butterflies were fluttering around in her belly.

She realized how long it had been since she had been alone with a man, and it had been longer than she cared to admit. Long enough that Candy would have certainly teased her about it.

"Hey, can I use your bathroom to change? I brought an extra set of clothes, just in case I got caught in this downpour," he asked, as he held up his backpack.

She thought, for just a moment, about when Candy had watched him in the locker room, and then realized she was probably scowling, so she quickly snapped herself out of it. He would eventually think she was crazy from her random facial expressions alone, if she didn't watch them.

"Yea, of course. I need to change too. Follow me."

Hazel led their way into the bedroom. Tate went into her bathroom to change while she rummaged through her closet, looking for something semi decent to wear, which was easier said than done. After getting into clean clothes, she went back into the kitchen to wait for him. The plan was to watch a movie and wait out the weather. Although it wasn't necessarily his ideal date for them, the weather had dictated differently.

She poured two glasses of red wine and then sat down on the sofa, setting the glasses on the coffee table in front of her. Determinedly, she had to stop herself from chewing on her fingernails while she waited but, fortunately, he didn't keep her waiting long. When Tate walked in, still rubbing his wet hair with a towel, wearing sweatpants and a tee shirt, he smiled coyly and took his place next to her on the sofa. At that moment, her nerves hit an all-time high. She could almost hear the crickets chirping within her head. She was so nervous she didn't know what to say. As she was trying to coax herself into talking, knowing how she would helplessly sit there in an awkward silence all night, he saved her from the trauma.

"Are you hungry?" he asked.

"Sure. Do you want to order takeout?"

"Or we could cook."

"Oh Tate, I'd have to bring you to the hospital."

He chuckled, reaching for her hand.

"Come on. Let's see what you've got in the kitchen. We can make something together."

"Okay, but it's your funeral," she joked, as she patted him on the back.

They walked into the kitchen, and he started digging through the refrigerator. He scratched at his chin, as though deep in thought, before putting ingredients onto the counter.

"What do you have there?"

"Well, you definitely need groceries... but we can make a mean grilled cheese. Sound good to you?"

"Actually, that sounds outstanding. I haven't had a grilled cheese since I was a kid. What do you want me to do?"

"Okay, so you can take out the skillet and melt a teaspoon of butter in it and I'll assemble the sandwiches."

"You've got it."

She bravely winked at him and started digging in the pot cabinet.

He pulled out four slices of bread and started assembling the sandwiches, layering them with mayonnaise, Colby and Provolone cheeses, and Dijon mustard. He placed them into the skillet and increased the fire, then he placed a heavier pot on top of them to flatten them down. She tried to move out of his way, but he wrapped his arm around her waist to keep her in the small kitchen with him. The care he took in preparing their dinner really impressed her. She did not know he liked to cook. That was one more domesticated skill he had over her. It admittedly made her feel a bit inadequate, which was her usual stance in life.

Once the sandwiches were ready, they plated them and sat down at her small kitchen table to eat. She was so hungry that she didn't wait long enough to take her first bite and singed her mouth on the hot cheese. The flavor was nostalgic for a time when she was a child. She had meant what she said about not having had grilled cheese since then, but she intended to have them more often moving forward. Tate ate his sandwich really quickly. She realized he had a lot of practice eating on the go from the inside of a police car.

"So, what kind of movie do you want to watch? Ghost movie?"

"Ha. Ha."

She couldn't tell from his face whether he was joking.

"Okay, action movie then," she offered.

"Great choice!"

They curled up on the couch and watched the movie. Afterwards, she flipped through a few more television shows, because she was stalling him before leaving. The rain continued to fall. She knew he intended to go home, but she really didn't want him to. She sat on the couch while he leaned over to put on his still damp shoes.

She wrestled with herself on whether she had the courage to be forward enough to tell him she wanted to be more to him than what they were. As they stood up so she could walk him to the door, she finally spoke up.

"I wish you didn't have to go," she said softly.

She grabbed his hand, intertwining their fingers.

He pressed his body against hers and ran his fingers gently over her cheek. With her face cradled in his hands, he pulled her into a kiss. All she could think about was how much she wanted him to stay with her, but she tried to ignore her racing thoughts so she could sink into the moment with him.

"I was going to head home, unless there was something else you had in mind?" he asked, with his forehead placed gently against hers.

She had never been so close to his eyes before, but it made her feel like she was falling. And with that closeness, that moment she couldn't just let pass her by, she leaned in and kissed him. She kissed him like she needed him, like she wanted only him. She didn't want him to leave, and she wanted him to know that. It was all the convincing he needed. He scooped her up and carried her into her bedroom, kicking off his shoes along the way.

Laying her onto the bed, he kissed her hungrily, as they ripped at each other's clothes, desperate to find a way out of them. Years of secretly wanting each other made the urgency all the more real as she clawed the muscles of his back, pulling him deeper into her. The heavy breaths in her ear and the smell of cedar and musk intoxicated her as her body fractured into a thousand electrified pieces.

She woke up the next morning to Tate smiling down at her. She self-consciously covered her face with the blanket, knowing she was being seen in full light, in a way he had never seen her before, but he popped his head under the blanket with her.

"You look beautiful. Why are you hiding from me?" he asked, his eyes bright with adoration.

"You're just saying that."

He kissed her softly on the lips and then rested his head on her shoulder. She closed her eyes as the chills coursed through her body.

"No, I'm not. I've always thought you were beautiful. It's time for you to realize that."

She uncovered her head and rested it on his chest, as he wrapped his arms around her.

"Hazel."

"Yea?"

"I love you. You know that, right?"

"I think I love you too," she said as he tucked

a stray hair behind her ear so he could kiss her cheek.

"Hello! Are you guys decent?" Candy called from the hallway.

"Come back later, Candy."

"Ooh, yea, okay. I'll be going then."

Candy's voice faded as she moved away from the door.

"Can we assume that she really left?" he asked, looking down at her curiously. He had one eyebrow raised, which made her blush.

"We can only hope. She has been hoping for a show."

* * *

Torrential downpours plagued the city for the following few days. The new lovers spent their free time curled up while watching movies. He insisted on helping her clean her apartment. Their relationship had progressed quickly, but it had been a long time in the making, so neither of them complained. Candy was delighted with the outcome, but Hazel forced her to leave the apartment when they needed privacy. Candy dramatically objected every time.

Raymond Waters' death was plastered all over the news, as was the news of the four female bodies that were found buried at his cabin. The police confirmed that he had murdered all of them. Protests erupted around his company's properties, so they had to shut down temporarily. Civil suits were filed to support the families of the victims.

Roy's mother had her heart surgery, and they expected her to make a full recovery. Since Roy had returned to living with her, he had been taking care of her. Also, with his reputation redeemed, he planned to look for a new job. Since the world of finance was spoiled permanently for him, he actually intended to apply to become a police officer.

Hazel woke up on the day of Angela's service feeling quite chipper. Although that may have seemed unsettling to some, she knew Angela was at peace, and she was excited to return Angela's necklace to her. Tate was off of work, so they planned to drive to Mobile together. She couldn't wait to see him, so she sent him a text as soon as she woke up.

"Can you be here for 11?"

She received an almost instantaneous response.

"Absolutely!"

Her cellular phone rang almost as soon as she received Tate's response.

"What should I wear?"

"Dress nice. See you then!"

"You got it, girl. Love you."

"Love you too."

She smiled when she hung up the phone and began getting herself ready for the trip.

When Tate arrived to pick her up, he swept her up in a hug and kiss the minute she opened the door.

"So, are you ready?" he asked, taking her bag.

"Yep. I think I finally need to say goodbye to my old friend."

Tate grabbed her hand and smiled.

"You did a good thing, Hazel. You'd better never put yourself in that much danger again, but you did a good thing."

The drive to Mobile for Angela's service was bittersweet. He drove while she played deejay and sang horribly. After her near-death ordeal, she'd promised herself that she would stop taking herself so seriously and start enjoying life. It had started with love and would continue from there.

Walking into Angela's memorial service, it was evident that she was loved. Angela's ex-husband, John, and her family had all turned up to pay their respects. Hazel let a small smile crawl across her lips when she saw Angela standing near the front of the church, smiling at all of her family and friends. She walked up to Angela's coffin and bowed her head to say a few words. Then she discreetly pulled the sapphire necklace out of her pocket and gently placed it on Angela's body.

"You can be at peace now, Angela. I figured you would want your grandmother's necklace back. Hopefully, this can help to guide you back home," Hazel whispered.

"Thank you," responded Angela, as she reached out to touch Hazel on the arm, attempting to give Hazel one more gentle squeeze before fading away.

They didn't stay at the service long and, instead, headed to dinner for their first proper date. Hazel had to give Candy the boot, so she and Tate could have some privacy for their meal, but Candy was more than happy to find something to entertain herself in a new city. They grabbed dinner at a Latin American restaurant in the downtown area called Roosters. It was actually her first time on an actual date in years. As close as she already was to Tate, she still felt nervous walking into the restaurant. The relationship was still so new, so she worried about filling those awkward silences she often left in conversations. Right next to a popular music venue, the restaurant itself looked to be very popular. Luckily, for Hazel, the background music filled the silences she couldn't fill by talking. It was something she needed to work on.

They had a slight wait for a table, so they sat on the benches outside and watched concert goers walk past sporting the shirts of their favorite bands. They had never heard of the band on the marquee sign, so they laughed while trying to guess its genre based on the appearances of their fans. The wait for a table seemed to go by quickly. Before they knew it, they had a table and were placing their order. The restaurant had a two for one deal on margaritas, so Tate insisted Hazel partake. Since he was the designated driver, she obliged. After the past few weeks, she figured she deserved it. After all the times she had foolishly turned him down, she was so glad she had finally said yes to going out with him. She felt good about their chances for the future.

The ride back to New Orleans was almost surreal. She had to pinch herself because of how lucky she felt. She was so sure that she was going to die not that long ago, but her luck had changed. She went from almost dying, to riding in a car, and holding hands with the man she had wanted to be with for a very long time. She didn't know what the future held, but she didn't intend to waste it.

She looked into the rear view mirror to see Candy in the backseat, making kiss faces at her and Tate. Candy was always a perverted joker, but she was a damn good friend. Better than any living friend, Hazel would bet. She stuck her tongue out at Candy, and Tate laughed. He was already getting used to the snarky spirit sidekick. He had no choice. They were both there to stay.

She was sad to see Tate go when he dropped her off at home, but she was wiped out. Plus, he had to work the next day. All she wanted was to take a shower, binge junk food, and watch Netflix until she passed out. Candy decided she would stay in with her that night, and she was glad for the company.

Once she got home, she took a shower, and then laid down on the sofa couch to watch reruns. She felt like she had turned over a new leaf in life, like she had grown so much from her ordeal with Raymond Waters. Knowing that the spirits would always come to her for help, she made a promise to herself, before drifting off to sleep, that she would never let them run her life again. It was the least she could do for those who loved her.

The Threat and the Murdered Man

"I am a powerful man, and you will pay for ruining me." His voice was a deep growl, but what struck me most was the hatred etched into a face I once knew well.

That face differed from how I remembered it. His eyes had turned as black as the darkness that surrounded him. A look of evil replaced what was once sophisticated and even handsome. He still wore the wounds he suffered the day he almost took my life.

Unable to move, I laid in utter horror as his battered body floated menacingly over me. I tried to scream, but no sound escaped. But I felt that scream inside me, and I knew it must have been showing through my eyes.

I fought back the urge to gag from the smell of rotted

flesh that lingered on his breath. I gasped as he lowered himself over me, before taking the air from my lungs. I struggled to fight... to choke out a sound.

"You have no control over me!" I sobbed, finally finding the strength to fight the attack, but I only heard a baleful laugh that hit me deep within my bones.

"I'm not going anywhere, Miss Watson. You will see me again."

***

Startled, Hazel woke up on the sofa in the comfort of her own apartment. Her breaths were still labored from the trauma of her nightmare and the apartment had grown frigid while she was sleeping. Rubbing her arms to help remove the chill, she glanced around the room for her spectral roommate, Candy, but did not see her.

Being a spirit, Candy did not need sleep, so it was not unusual for her to roam the city while Hazel slept. There was plenty to look at in the city of New Orleans, especially at night. Severe weather did not seem to bother Candy either, so the night's show would not have kept her inside.

Meanwhile, the storm had knocked the power out, so Hazel stumbled her way to the kitchen, so she could look for a flashlight. Flashes of lightning temporarily lit her way while sheets of rain beat against the windows. Finding a flashlight, she walked back to the sofa and sat down.

Although the weather outside was torrential, the apartment was fairly quiet. Setting the flashlight on the coffee table, she resolved to sit there and hope the power would come back on quickly, or that Candy would return to give her company. Hazel's boyfriend and New Orleans' police officer, Tate Cormier, had gone home after their recent out-of-town trip, because he had an early shift, so she did not want to call and wake him. Lying against the armrest, she began scrolling through pictures on her phone, hoping the boredom would eventually put her back to sleep.

An unnerving sound startled her upright. She thought she could hear rapid breathing, but the sound was not coming from her. Looking around the room, she only saw darkness. Her chest tightened as her anxiety rose.

"Candy, is that you?"

She called out, just in case Candy was somewhere else in the apartment, unbeknownst to her. She listened quietly, but heard no response. The breath sounds increased in volume, synchronizing with the sound of her own heartbeat in her ears.

Flicking the flashlight on, she stood up from the sofa and faced the direction of the sound. She hoped to see nothing, but gasped when a figure rose from the darkness. A man, who appeared to be in his late twenties, was bleeding in the corner of her living room.

Her hand trembled as it gripped the flashlight, causing him to flicker in and out of view. His barely solid presence told her he was not a living man, but a spirit and, judging from the state of his body, he had not died a natural death. He had been murdered.

She approached him cautiously, although she could taste the fear in her throat, making her mouth dry. Something about him looked familiar, and she tried to get a better look at him, but he was not in a recognizable state. It was too dark, and he was soaking wet. He did not speak, but his eyes followed her movements.

"What's your name? I can help you."

She forced her voice to come out calm, although she was anything but. She may have helped spirits since she was a child, but it never got easy to have them invade her personal space. He continued to watch her, but he did not respond.

Maybe he's in shock... do ghosts experience shock?

Wearing only boxer shorts and socks, his body shivered violently. The stab wounds were all over him, and they bled profusely, although he no longer had a corporeal form. There was no question... whoever had stabbed him had fully intended to take his life, and they had succeeded.

Without warning, Candy rushed past her, pulling the man's spirit into a tight embrace.

"Jake! Who did this to you?" Candy screamed.

Afterword

If you liked this book, please leave a review on Amazon and Good reads! Thank you!

***

Justice for the Slain (A Hazel Watson Mystery Book 2), is available NOW!

After surviving an abduction and near death herself, Hazel, along with her police officer boyfriend, Tate, and Candy, are looking forward to their brand of normalcy.

But the spirit of a murdered man shows up in Hazel's apartment. He's not just any man, however. He's the man Candy was murdered over. This, once again, throws their world into chaos, causing her to rethink what had never been questioned.

Did the police have the right man in prison?

Hazel tests powers she never knew she had and finds herself caught up in a tangled case of obsession and murder. The more she navigates the killer's past, the more entangled her life becomes, until it endangers those she loves. Forced to put those closest to her in the line of fire, Hazel marches into the dangerous world of a psychotic killer, to put their havoc to an end before it's too late.

***

The Prequel, *Kindred Spirits*, is available on paperback and Kindle Unlimited!

Candy Townsend enjoyed her life as a young bartender in the city of New Orleans. Sure, she had a complicated relationship with her ex-boyfriend, Brad, but she was in love with a new man and was hopeful for the future. Sadly, her life, and her future, changed forever after one fateful night. Candy struggled in her new state of being until nearly a year later when a young woman with a special ability entered her apartment. A young woman named Hazel Watson.

Hazel Watson had newly graduated from law school and it was time for her to move into her own apartment and join the adult world. Something she was admittedly dreading. Unfortunately, the only place she could afford in the popular city of New Orleans had a reputation for being haunted. Undeterred, and desperate to find a place of her own, she moved in regardless. Using her hereditary ability to communicate with the dead, she befriends her new apartment's resident ghost and teams up with the feisty spirit to help other lost souls she encounters.

***

A *Hazel Watson Mystery Book 3*, Whispers from the Swamp, is available NOW!

Many changes are happening in the life of Hazel Watson... good changes... but the demands of the spirit world remain the same. The exhausting, stressful obligations she's dealt with since she was a child. It's inescapable.

So, when the bodies of two women are discovered in the swamps of South Louisiana, the people of New Orleans are shocked... but not Hazel. She had been seeing the faces of those same two women in her dreams for weeks, haunting her and beckoning her to find their killer.

Having never been comfortable with sharing the nature of her abilities with others, Hazel struggles with having to do just that when she receives a ghostly warning about the impending abduction of another woman.

Can Hazel overcome her fear of being exposed, and of the swamp itself, before more women fall victim to the killer who stalks the Louisiana wetlands?

Acknowledgements

Thank you, mom, for letting me read this book to you, although the story was continuously interrupted by my swearing every time I had to stop and fix an error that I missed during my first 50 edits. Thank you for being there for me! I love you!

***

Thank you to my husband, Trevor, for not annoying me as much as usual, so that I could have time to write, and for cooking those Hello Fresh meals so that I didn't starve. I appreciated the breakfasts too! I love you!

***

Thank you to my amazing friend, DJ, for editing

this book, although I kept editing it at the same time, and sending you new versions almost daily.

***

Thank you to my amazing Mother-in-Law, Wendy, for helping to edit this book, even when you were on vacation. I know that you could have been kayaking. Love you very much!

***

Thank you to author, Jenna Moreci, for your amazing YouTube channel and Skillshare classes. I know that I'm not the only writer who had a dream of becoming a published author, but was intimidated, until we came across you! Your YouTube channel has not only made me laugh my ass off, but has also taught me so much, and gave me the courage that I needed to 'write the damn book,' so thank you! Oh, and your Savior series ROCKS! I've already read it twice.

***

Thank you to author, E.E. Holmes, for inspiring

me with your Gateway series, and being open to chatting with me, through Facebook messenger, when I first began this journey. You've grown into a great friend! The Gateway series was the first paranormal fiction series that I read since I was a teen, and it blew my mind. I knew it was where I needed to be. It was what I needed to read, and it was what I needed to write. Thank you so much for creating that world. It meant more than you know. If I could make one request..., could we please get another book? I just miss the gang so much!

***

Thank you to author, H.P. Bayne, for not only inspiring me with your amazing Sullivan Gray series, but also for responding to my messages and giving me all the advice that I asked for. I consider you to be a friend, and I appreciate everything that you have done to help me on this journey. And, as I've said before, as long as you write them, I'll read them!

***

Thank you to author, George Mann, for the signed Newbury & Hobbes books after my youngest daughter's open-heart surgery. They were meant for her but I loved them! They really got me into the paranormal mystery genre and influenced my own sleuthing character.

***

Thank you to all of my readers! I hope that you all enjoyed this first book of Hazel's story. This first novel was such an amazing learning experience for me, but I'm taking all that I have learned, and am putting all of it into Hazel's stories that follow. I can't wait for you to read about Hazel's next mystery in the sequel, Justice for the Slain, coming soon!

Meet the Author

C. A. Varian was raised in Lockport, Louisiana, into an often-low-income household. She spent a lot of her childhood fishing, crabbing, and playing school. She loved pretending to be the teacher and assigning work to her cousins. Her love of reading started very young, where she used to complete several books per week in elementary school so she could earn a free personal pizza from Pizza Hut. Even once free pizzas were no longer an option, she still steadily read novels, usually above the reading level for her age group, and loved visiting the library to stock up on books. She started writing poetry and short stories while still in junior high through high school, although she stopped writing, at least for fun, once she had children and went to college. Thankfully, her writing hiatus ended, and she resumed her love for writing.

She earned a Bachelor of Arts degree, as well as a Master's degree in History. She also worked towards getting her teaching certification. She did almost all of her college education while also being the mother of two children. After graduating from college, she began teaching public school, a career she continues to this day, currently teaching special education at a local middle school.

She's married to a retired military officer, so she spent many years moving around for his career, but they now live in central Alabama, with her youngest daughter, Arianna. Her oldest daughter, Brianna, no longer lives at home and is engaged to be married. She has two Shih Tzus she considers her children. Boy, Charlie, and girl, Luna, are their mommy's shadows. She also has three cats: Ramses, Simba, and Cookie, as well as five chickens and two ducks.

Made in the USA
Columbia, SC
10 June 2022

61496338R00193